People for Lunch

People for Lunch

Georgina Hammick

Methuen

First published in Great Britain 1987
by Methuen London Ltd
11 New Fetter Lane, London EC4P 4EE
Copyright © Georgina Hammick 1987

Printed and bound in Great Britain
by Redwood Burn Limited, Trowbridge, Wiltshire

British Library Cataloguing in Publication Data

Hammick, Georgina
    People for lunch
    I. Title
    823′ .914[F] PR6058.A554/

    ISBN 0-413-14900-5

Acknowledgements
The title story was a winner of
Stand Magazine's 1985 Short Story Competition,
and appeared in the Winter 1985–6 issue of *Stand*.
Mad About The Boy was first published
in *Fiction Magazine* and included in *Best of
Fiction Magazine* (Dent paperback 1986).
A Few Problems in the Day Case Unit was published
in the Autumn 1986 number of *Critical Quarterly*.
The quotation from 'Return to Sender' is
used by permission of Carlin Music Corp.
The quotation from 'The Shadow Play' by
Noel Coward is used by permission of
Methuen London Ltd.

In Memoriam
F.M.T. and A.A.N-S.

Contents

The Tulip Plate

'There's a man I often see here,' Nell said, as she walked round the lake with her weekend visitor. 'No matter what time of day I choose – on Saturdays and Sundays, that is – he's nearly always here too.'

'How romantic,' said her visitor, whose name was Margaret and who was interested in men. 'What sort of man? Perhaps he has conceived a passion for you.'

'No,' Nell said, referring to the words romantic and passion. 'I don't know what sort of man. It's his dog I'm interested in – you don't see so many white bull-terriers about these days.'

Margaret said she wouldn't know a bull-terrier if she met one. She had to be honest about it, she'd never liked dogs or trusted them. Presumably, if it was fully white, it must be albino and have pink eyes?

Nell said yes to this and notched up one more thing they didn't have in common. To prove the point she called out 'Hurry up, Dearest!' to her own dog who was busy in the reeds, looking for water rats.

They had to keep moving because of the cold. The lake was a large one for southern England and, with its inlets and varied vegetation, gave the appearance of being natural, when it was man-made. Three quarters of the way round it ran a metalled path-cum-roadway, wide enough for single motor traffic, on the waterside of which creosoted wood stumps, like dwarf telegraph poles, had been set at intervals to deter cars from parking on the bank. They were having to stick to this path and not venture into the woods that bordered its other side because Nell, writing to confirm train times, had omitted to tell Margaret to bring boots.

'I should have told you to bring some boots,' she said, 'so that we could walk in the woods.'

'I don't own any boots,' Margaret said. 'I never walk at home if I can help it – except to go to the shops, of course. But I'm quite enjoying this,' she added, understanding suddenly that her truthfulness, of which ordinarily she was not ashamed, might just occasionally be mistaken for rudeness. 'It reminds me of the Round Pond in Kensington Gardens.'

'North America, more like' – Nell was astounded by such inaccuracy – 'or Canada to be precise. Look.' She stopped, and Margaret stopped, and they both stared beyond a slatted landing stage across the dull water to where nameless waterfowl skied and flapped, and to where, in the far distance, little boats with coloured sails raced in the wind. On the opposite bank a mixed forest, dominated by giant pines or firs, climbed into the sky, and beneath it, right on the shore line, they could just make out a log cabin with a flagpole jutting from its roof. This was the sailing club, Nell explained. 'You see,' she said, 'it's not like England at all. It makes me think – especially when the sky's a really bright blue – of those photographs in the *National Geographic*.' She was pleased with this piece of observation, and used some version of it to the infrequent visitors she brought to the lake, most of whom were in wholehearted agreement.

'So it is! How clever of you!'

'You're absolutely right – we could be on Golden Pond! Did you see that film, by the way?'

Margaret, however, merely shivered and nodded in the direction of the boats and remarked, 'Red sails in the sunset,' in a dry voice.

'Have you had enough?' Nell felt she had to ask. Margaret's clothes were too thin and smart for a cold country walk. But what was she going to do with her if they turned back so soon? Tea would be a bit of a diversion, but after that? They had no friends in common anymore. What would they find to talk about for the rest of the evening?

The night before, the day of Margaret's arrival and first visit for nearly twenty years, they had talked shop. Or rather Margaret – following Nell from sitting room to kitchen, from kitchen to cellar, from fridge to cooker, while breathing down her neck or standing on her toes (and Nell was a claustrophobe) had talked shop, and Nell had interjected the odd 'yes, but,' or 'don't you think – '. But if there is a limit to how long two persons – the one a librarian, the other a bookseller, the former doing most of the talking, the latter most of the listening – can maintain an enthusiastic discourse on stock-control systems and library cuts, Public Lending Right and the Net Book Agreement, they had reached it; if there is a point when analysis of sales and borrowings, a debate on the problem of unreturned books and shoplifting ('They're both theft, mind you, straightforward theft, and should be punished as such,' Margaret had exclaimed, with a jerk of her elbow that had sent a china candlestick flying), becomes less than enthralling, then ditto. Even the topics they were agreed upon – the rudeness of customers, the inefficiency of publishers, the vanity of authors ('They never come into the shop to buy, you know,' Nell said when she could get a word in, 'merely to check that their own dreary books are on the shelf') – had lost their edge by midnight. 'Must hit the hay now, folks,' Margaret had announced in what she thought of as an American accent, 'or I won't have gotten my beauty sleep.'

For Nell, the worst aspect of the evening had been the discovery that Margaret did not drink or smoke. She'd made one small glass of sherry last nearly two hours, drumming the table lightly with manicured fingers each time Nell reached for the whisky bottle or for her cigarettes. On the other hand – and it seemed odd in one so thin and birdlike – she had an enormous appetite for food. Nell had imagined the cottage pie would do at least two meals, but Margaret – 'Do you mind if I do? It seems a pity to waste it' –had helped herself three times until nothing remained but a spoonful of mashed potato. The fruit salad had disappeared likewise. When

Margaret finally put down her spoon, a solitary slice of banana was left swimming in the bowl.

The problem of what to have for supper now beset Nell as they passed two umbrellas, all that could be seen of two fishermen wedged below them on the bank. Perhaps if she were to open a tin of baked beans and another of mushrooms, and fry an onion or two . . .

'I'm game to go a bit further,' Margaret said. She always made the best of things. And she felt no inducement to return to Nell's freezing house and sit, as they had yesterday evening and this morning, in Nell's squalid sitting room in front of Nell's pathetic fire. Also, Nell had threatened her with a tour of the garden. It was incomprehensible to Margaret how gardeners could stand around in cold and mud and enthuse – and expect others to enthuse – over a collection of dead and indistinguishable twigs. 'Do you enjoy cooking?' she asked, to cover the loudness of her shoes and Nell's boots on the tarmac. The digestion of a pub lunch of bread and cheese was not being helped by the memory of last night's grey mince, and what could only have been instant mashed potato.

'Not in the ordinary way,' Nell said. She stopped briefly to pierce a last year's oak leaf with the spike of her walking stick. 'But I like doing it for special occasions.'

Margaret wondered which category her own visit came into. 'I love it,' she said, with an emphasis that made it sound a virtue. 'I enjoy my food, I'm not ashamed to admit. Planning meals, shopping for them, preparing them – surely one of the great pleasures of life.'

Nell yawned and said nothing.

'Is that your man?' Margaret asked, as they stepped to the verge to avoid collision with a young-looking father and two children in red anoraks. The bigger child, his head thrust forward and over the handlebars, made motorbike noises and zig-zagged his tricycle; the smaller one hung over the side of his pushchair and scraped a stick along the tarmac.

'Aggression starts early in the male,' Nell said to no one in particular. 'No, he's always alone – except for his bull-terrier, that is. He's not my man, incidentally.' They climbed down from the bank, but Margaret lingered for a moment in the road, looking over her shoulder and repeating 'Boys will be boys' in an admiring voice.

They walked on in silence. A pale sunshine, that had been struggling all day with the clouds, gave up, and the afternoon grew increasingly dark and wild. It was the end of March and officially spring, but there was no sign yet of green and growing things. Margaret folded her arms and hugged the chest of her Country Casuals coat. She was ready to go back. Not back to Nell's, but back on the train to her own tidy and centrally-heated flat, and the prospect of supper – sole *bonne femme,* perhaps, with croquette potatoes and braised celery hearts.

'That's it – we'll have to turn round now,' Nell said, eyeing Margaret's shoes. A few yards ahead of them the road dwindled into a waterlogged track, winding between alders bent double in the wind. She swung the dog lead round her head and whistled for Dearest who was doing her best to follow a squirrel into a tree.

It was after they'd turned round, with the wind in their backs now instead of their faces, that things began to improve between them.

'Do you remember Miss Benson?' Nell suddenly asked.

'Miss Benson,' Margaret repeated, 'Miss Benson? *Joan* Benson. Oh dear. I never thought to hear that name again.' And she started to laugh.

'She was in love with Elaine Crabtree,' Nell went on, 'when Elaine was hockey captain and head girl.' Nell remembered this because she'd been in love with Elaine Crabtree herself. Elaine had had an oval, freckled face and untidy eyebrows she combed in front of the glass with a pocket comb kept for the purpose. Margaret, who hadn't loved anyone at school apart from Shelley, didn't remember this detail, but she could see Miss Benson and Elaine, in particular the former's thighs as she belted down the pitch, blowing her whistle and shouting, 'Reds, get free! Mark your opponent, Sally!'

'Miss Benson was sacked, you know,' Nell said, 'shortly after we left. I can't remember who told me. She was found on the hockey field in the middle of the night, dead drunk apparently and singing bawdy songs.'

'You're making it up,' Margaret said. But she was pleased with the turn their conversation had taken.

The memory of Miss Benson led them on to other members of staff and other girls, to school buildings and classrooms and dormitories, to the prefects' study and 'Pre's Teas' of cold baked beans and condensed milked sucked from the tin. Prompting and correcting each other, they were able to conjure up the jacaranda trees that bordered the drive, the wood smoke ('That smell,' Nell said, 'I keep it here, at the back of my nose'), curling into the sky from the staff bandas that lay below the games fields in an exclusive cluster out of sight of the main block. They recalled mornings that, because they were six thousand feet above sea level, remained coldly misted until midday, afternoons so wiltingly hot that failure to wear a hat was punished by an order mark or with sunstroke.

'She must be dead now,' Margaret said. She was speaking of the biology mistress, whose luxuriant moustache and habit of throwing chalk at her pupils they had just been dissecting. 'Very probably, they're all dead. It's nearly forty years ago, you realize.'

This terrible truth brought them both to a halt. What have I done with my life? Nell thought, What have I got to show for all these years? On an impulse, she put her arm through Margaret's, regretted it at once, and had to leave it there.

'Quiz time, now,' Margaret said, encouraged by the intimacy Nell's arm betokened. 'What did we sing in that inter-school choral comp we were expected to win and came bottom of?'

'A La-a-ake and a faer-ie boat,' Nell sang, 'and something else. Can't remember what. Oh yes I can – in Hans' old mill his five black cats – '

'Three black cats.'

' – his three black cats watch the bins for the thieving rats –

16

Jekyll and Jessup, and o-one eye-eyed – help.'

'Jill,' Margaret said.

'Jill. Cats are never Jill though, are they. Supposing they were, someone called Hans would have cats called Gretchen or Gertrud. Why are children made to sing such nonsense? A lake and a fairy boat – I ask you.'

'We are walking beside a lake,' Margaret pointed out, 'and the fairy boats are over there.' But when they scanned the water, the boats were somewhere beyond a promontary and hidden from them by the trees.

A sudden cloudburst of hailstones sent them running down the bank to a rustic bench and the shelter of a yew tree. The yew formed a black tent above their heads, and they sat cosily together watching the hailstones tear the surface of the lake.

'What's that scent you're wearing?' Nell said. It came from Margaret's silk scarf, and the collar of her coat. It was strong, and in some way unsettling: she never wore scent herself.

'*Jolie Madame,*' Margaret said. 'How do we stop your dog whining? Does he do it all the time?' Nell picked up Dearest and held her on her knee, where she dug her claws in and trembled and continued to whine. A reek of wet dog displaced the *Jolie Madame.*

'Odeur de wet dog,' Margaret said. She turned her head away. She turned back to Nell. 'You weren't very nice at school,' she confided, poking her in the ribs. 'I hated you at the beginning.'

'*We* thought *you* were too big for your boots,' Nell said, recalling how Margaret, whose father had been a major or colonel in some regiment sent out from England to put down the Mau Mau, had arrived in the middle of a Lent term and gone – at only fifteen – straight into the sixth form. She'd made the rest of them – settlers' daughters like herself, whose parents farmed in remote up-country places, District Commissioners' daughters, daughters of doctors and dentists and government officials in Nairobi – feel that 'colonial' equalled not just naive and unsophisticated, but stupid. Nell couldn't remember now how they'd ever become friends. Perhaps on her own side, it had been a question of finding when you couldn't beat someone, that it might be expedient to join them.

Margaret reminded Nell that she's never owned any boots. She asked if Nell missed Africa in general, and the farm at Hoey's Bridge in particular, and Nell said she did, and more and more as she got older. But she'd never go back, she said, never. They talked about Hoey's Bridge for a while. Margaret remembered playing pingpong in the creamery and how green and cold it was in there compared to outside, and how they'd been caught once by Nell's mother dipping their fingers in the vats. She had a clear picture of Nell's mother, she said, in mens' brown trousers and an aertex shirt and bush hat; in fact she was prepared to swear Nell's mother hadn't worn anything else during the whole of her visit, which must have been three weeks. She remembered being woken every morning by the shamba boys sweeping the tennis court and singing, if you could call it that; and she remembered a tennis party with twin brothers who'd come from Kitale for the weekend, and how rude and cocky they were, especially the smaller one who had ginger hair.

Nell wondered if it was working in a library that made Margaret talk so much. She watched the storm ending. Like a cine film run backwards, the hail was drawn off the lake and back up into the clouds. Afterwards the banks, the bushes and the rough grass at the water's edge were left with a granular coating, like imitation snow.

'Behold, a white dog,' Margaret said when they were back on the roadway. 'It must be your man at last.'

'Yes, that's him.' A long way off, a man and a dog could just be seen heading in their direction. 'Since you're so interested in what you insist on calling *my* man, I dare you,' said Nell, on whom all this chat about school and childhood had had the effect of making her feel frivolous and fifteen, 'to say something when we meet. Engage him in conversation.'

'Whatever for?' said Margaret. But she was intrigued, nevertheless.

'Because,' said Nell, 'because it would be amusing. I'd like to

18

know what his voice is like. I imagine it to be Scots – Edinburgh, not Glasgow.'

Margaret said it would make more sense if Nell spoke to him because she was the one who saw him all the time. But Nell said no. She didn't explain that it was too late to speak to anyone with whom she had not even exchanged nods. He always looked preoccupied and unapproachable, his eyes on the ground or on the lake. Even their dogs avoided each other. She had no grounds for approaching him. But Margaret didn't care who she said Boo to. 'You could say "Good evening",' Nell told her, 'and perhaps something about his dog. You could say "that's a handsome dog – is he a Staffordshire bull-terrier?" – I happen to know that he is, but it's a legitimate question to dog owners. We enjoy compliments and enquiries,' she added pointedly.

'I'm not fond of dogs, as you know,' Margaret said. As she spoke, and as if to confirm her opinion, Dearest defecated hugely and wetly on the grass beside them, afterwards stretching out her back legs and kicking up a shower of slush and mud.

'Talk about the weather then,' Nell said. 'If you do it,' she encouraged, 'if you can keep him talking for at least five minutes, I'll let you have the tulip plate.'

The evening before, Margaret had admired the plate that had contained her cottage pie. It had a pattern of intertwined red and yellow tulips round the rim, and in the centre, once the mince and potato and watery beans had been forked up, she'd discovered a wicker basket with red and yellow tulips springing from it. 'What a very pretty plate!' she'd said. 'Is it part of a set?' Nell, who thought the design feeble and the colours crude, had merely shrugged and smiled.

Nell's offer acted as a spur to Margaret. If the plate were hers – she'd even decided this as Nell took it away and put it in the sink – it would hang on the sitting-room wall. She had just the right spot for it, in a little alcove above the bookcase. And it would go with the curtains which, while neither red nor yellow, had splashes of both in their multicoloured pattern.

19

'I'll see then,' she said to Nell. 'I won't promise, but I might.' A sense of conspiracy quickened their footsteps. As her quarry came nearer, Margaret tried to size him up, but he kept getting lost behind the trees, or hidden by a curve in the lake, and when he was visible she couldn't see his face because he was looking at the ground. He'd evidently not sheltered from the storm, for as he came into focus she could see that his hair was sopping and flattened to his scalp. The dog was wet through, also: a pink piggy skin showed through his saturated coat. A hideous creature, surely, even by dog lovers' standards: tiny pink eyes, a pink belligerent nose, wet fat slapping as he rolled rather than walked –

It was at this moment, when they were perhaps fifty yards from certain encounter, that a car, going too fast for the place and the weather, overtook them, its tyres sending out a burst of grit and slush. Margaret's camel coat, her twelve denier tights, her tan court shoes, took the worst of it. Cursing, she bent down to examine the damage. Nell seized her by the elbow.

'Don't bother with that now,' she said. 'It'll brush off when it's dry.' But Margaret was no longer in the mood for schoolgirl games. She kept swivelling to see the back of her coat. It was wrecked; from what she could see of it, a major disaster.

'Go on, go on, cowardy custard,' Nell said out of the side of her mouth. But as they came face to face with 'her' man, it was Nell who was the coward. She stepped well clear of the confrontation and made for the trees with Dearest, neck fur up and tail down between her legs, at her heels. Abandoned on the tarmac, Margaret hesitated for a moment, and then went up to the man and stood in front of him so that he was forced to stop and look at her. He had pale blue eyes and a tired face, but it was a much younger face than Margaret had been expecting. Nell had said nothing about his being a young man. He couldn't have been more than thirty, at the most.

'Good afternoon,' she began, and stopped. Out of the corner of her eye she could see Nell, some way ahead and out of earshot, pretending an interest in a larch cone she'd found in the grass. A question about the bull-terrier, at that moment sniffing her shoes and ankles and the hem of her coat, a comment on the freakishness of the storm, half formed themselves, retreated, evaporated altogether. She had nothing to say to this fellow at all. She opened her mouth. 'Tell me, how is Mary?' she heard herself say.

The man looked at her, and it was a look more curious than surprised. He swivelled his head and looked up at the sky, and then back at Margaret. To her alarm, his eyes filled with large, blistery tears.

'Not so good today,' he said in a sad, flat voice. 'It can't be long now, she's very weak.' He blinked, and the tears tipped out of his eyelids and broke on his cheeks. He brushed them away with the back of his hand. 'She sleeps most of the day, when the pain lets her.' He nodded towards the bull-terrier. 'I'm taking a little breather with Tray.'

'I'm so sorry,' Margaret said, appalled. She'd never seen a man cry.

'If only she'd fought more,' the man said, 'if only she'd put up a proper fight – ' his voice tailed off. He clenched his fists and stared out at the lake. 'But you know Mary,' he said, turning back to Margaret with a sad smile, 'she's always been a fatalist. She just accepts things.'

'I'm so sorry,' Margaret said.

'Thank you,' the man said. 'I suppose you work at the Centre,' he added – and it seemed to Margaret to be not a question, but a statement requiring only her confirmation – 'with Janet and the others.'

'Yes,' Margaret nodded, 'yes I do.'

'Janet has been a particular help,' the man said. His emphasis made Margaret feel that she herself had not been. 'She's sitting with Mary now, reading to her, holding her hand.'

'That's good,' Margaret said. 'I'm glad about that.' She stepped backwards and then sideways, to give him a chance to walk on, but he didn't take it.

'Give her my love, please,' she said. She put out a hand and touched his sleeve. It was soaking. 'Goodbye,' she said. 'God bless you.'

'Whom shall I say?' the man called after her. 'Whose love shall I give?'

'Alison's,' Margaret said, over her shoulder, without looking back.

'Alison's,' the man repeated, 'Alison's.' He watched her walk slowly away from him, her shoulders hunched, her head bowed, the posture – at once reverent and self-conscious – of one who has just left the altar rail after receiving Communion.

'Well,' Nell said impatiently, coming out of her ambush, 'you've won the tulip plate, I see. You were hours – I nearly died of cold.'

'It was awful,' Margaret said, more to herself than to Nell. 'I walked into some sort of family tragedy.'

'Must be his wife who's dying,' Nell said when Margaret, haltingly, and omitting the 'Alison' and the 'God bless you' her thirty-year-old atheism was still smarting from, had recounted the conversation. 'Cancer, I should think, from the sound of it.'

All lies, Margaret murmured wonderingly to herself, one lie after another, I told him nothing but lies.

'Or one of his children,' Nell said. 'The Centre could be a day nursery, or a clinic, or a home for handicapped children.' And she was silent, trying to imagine what it would be like to have a child; a healthy child, a sick child, a child you loved and who loved you; a child who died. If it was me dying, she thought suddenly, who would weep? Would anyone?

'I still don't understand,' she began as they reached the car, 'what – ' She was going to say, what made you ask about *Mary*?, but knew that however she phrased it, it would sound like the question that really occupied her, which was: How could something so strange happen to someone as insensitive as Margaret? And why should a man she'd seen countless times on her walks, and who'd never so much as glanced in her direction, choose Margaret, of all people, to tell his troubles to?

She opened the rear door to find her shoes, and then leant against the car while she took off her boots. Margaret got into the passenger seat without saying a word, and did up her seat belt.

Nell didn't like this silent Margaret. Silence was the prerogative of the imaginative. Moreover, this silence had a secret, exclusive feel. 'A cup of tea is what we need, Meg,' she said, switching on the engine. 'It'll cheer you up. I hope.'

But Margaret did not cheer up. (Something momentous had happened, something that would alter her life. She had been chosen, she knew. But for what? For what?) She sat stiffly in her ruined coat, and stared ahead as the windscreen wipers raked and squeaked.

'Just going to see if they've got any tea-cakes, then,' Nell said crossly, pulling up without warning outside the village shop – an action which provoked a swerve, a blast on the horn and a rude gesture from the driver behind.

A Few Problems in the Day Case Unit

My name is Lettice Pomfrey and I am thirty-four years old. I am sitting in the gynaecologist's waiting room waiting to see the gynaecologist. I tell you this now, at the beginning, in case gynaecology is not the subject for you; in case you find some aspects of it distasteful; in case you would rather be somewhere else than in this waiting room on a hot and sunny July afternoon.

I don't want to be here; I've a high failure rate in gynaecologists. The first one I saw was a misogynist and an extortionist, the second a lecher. The third one might have been all right, I can't positively say he wasn't, but we moved house before I had a chance to find out. The fourth one, Mr Gamble, I haven't yet met. He's been recommended by my doctor and by several people I know who variously say he's sympathetic, attractive, dishy. A surgeon's wife I share the school run with told me Mr G. is the envy of his colleagues, who've had to watch him sweep the gynaecological board, not just of the county's childbearers, but of the menopausal. They seek him out, according to her, for hysterectomies, for removal of ovarian cysts and ovaries, and for Hormone Replacement Therapy. This is enough to put me off him, but I'm telling myself to keep an open mind.

The waiting room is in the consulting rooms an ENT man, a paediatrician and Mr Gamble share. They see their private patients here, and their NHS patients at the Infirmary. I'd have been quite happy, not being on BUPA, to see Mr G. at the NHS clinic he holds on Tuesdays, but my doctor explained that because of the consultants' dispute, and as I can't be called an urgent case, it'd

27

mean tagging on to the end of a long waiting list. Impossible to say when I'd get an appointment. It could be years, not months. Centuries even, my doctor said, with one of his occasional flashes of humour. Milleniums.

The waiting room is very smart. Its colour scheme is white and fawn and chocolate brown. The ceiling is white, the walls fawn, the carpet fawn with a chocolate Greek key pattern round the edge. The chairs are white tubular with chocolate wool seats. There are two rubber plants, one either side of the fireplace, standing in white, square jardinières. In front of the plate-glass window is a large table with a glass top, and on this are magazines. They've been arranged like a game of giant clock patience, but in the centre, where the king of hearts or spades should be, is an enormous ashtray, square and glass to match the table. I would like a cigarette at this moment, but don't want to be caught smoking. Also it seems common courtesy to keep my breath sweet for Mr Gamble, even if my mouth is not the part of me he'll be seeing most of.

Apart from the furniture, the waiting room is empty. I walk up and down, try out different chairs and angles, tidy a thumbnail, sniff the magazines. These are new, or recent, issues of glossy monthlies; no stimulating reads here, no *Diver* or *Motorcycling Weekly* or *Aircraft Modeller*; no *Exchange & Mart*. The only mag on this table that could be called specialist is *Horse and Hound*. The number I've got hold of contains a round-up of last year's hunting season, with copious photographs. A Good Day Out With The Whitemore Vale, I read. Colonel Jim Vane-Fitzpatrick, joint master, shows hounds –

Mrs Pomfrey, ready for you now.

The nurse who's come for me is a dark girl, and pretty except for some serious and disconcerting spots (no matter how often you come across them, spotty nurses, like dentists with bad breath and hairdressers with hacked hair, are always somehow shocking). I follow her to a little room where I am weighed, and where my blood pressure is taken. As she pumps me up I squinny to see the reading, but she's too quick for me. That's fine, she says grimly, unwinding the black mackintosh from my arm.

Mrs Pomfrey for you, Mr Gamble, she says, opening a connecting door. Mr Gamble gets up from behind his desk and comes forward and shakes my hand. Then he squeezes my shoulder, a gentle pressure that encourages me to sit down on the chair my side of the desk and facing his chair. When he has returned to his place he leans towards me on his elbows.

Well, Mrs Pomfrey, he says, well now.

Mr Gamble is a good-looking man; he may even be attractive. Somebody told me he's a bit like James Stewart, and he is, about the mouth and chin. His eyes aren't blue though, they're brown. They're kind eyes, and the expression in them of sympathy and concern is intensified by the furrows in his brow. They cannot be a misogynist's eyes. I'm sure. And there's no hint of lechery in them.

Mr G. begins to ask me questions – my date of birth; my husband's date of birth; the dates of birth and sexes of our four children, etc. – the answers to which he jots down with a fountain pen on a sheet of unlined A4. I wonder why he bothers with this: most of the information must be in the letter from my doctor I can see on his desk, or in the file containing my medical notes, ditto. Perhaps he hasn't read the letter or had time to glance through the notes; or perhaps he prefers to do his own spadework in what for him is new ground, in what for me is old ground, dug over many times before.

How old was I, Mr G. wants to know, when I had my first period? Can I give him a brief account of the births of my children? Am I a smoker? Do I have any problems at all with bowels or waterworks?

Mr G. lays his pen on the paper. Would I like to tell him, and I can take my time, about the various methods of birth control I and my husband have tried during the course of our marriage? We started off with my using a cap, I tell him, and Mr G. picks up his pen and writes Diaphragm on the sheet of paper. Then we started a

29

baby – on purpose, I explain, and then after the baby was born I went on the pill. Oral C, Mr G. writes down. And how did that suit? he asks, leaning forward again.

The truth is it made me sick and fat and gave me headaches, and I tell him this. Mr G. writes, Usual side effects and something else I can't read. Sounds as though you should have been on a low dose pill, he says. I was, I assure him, on the lowest dose available at the time. And after the second baby? After our second baby I tried a Coil. I.U.D., Mr G. writes. Will I describe for him, if I can, this Coil? It looked like a firework, I tell him, you know, a squib. Ah, I *see*, Mr G. says, rubbing his chin, How did that work for you? Were you happy with it? I hesitate – but what is the point of mincing words? He's asking me, after all; he wants to know. I got the curse very badly, I tell him, every ten days. And I had a dragging, stitching pain, low down. Heavy loss, Mr G. writes, Discomfort. And after the third baby? Another pill, same side effects. And after the fourth (which I've already told him was a mistake, and which he has decided was unplanned)? Another Coil, a different sort, with the same results only more so. It became embedded, I explain, and for them to remove it I had to spend a day in hospital and have a general anaesthetic . . . .

You don't seem to have much luck, do you? Mr G. still sounds concerned, but at the same time ever so slightly disbelieving, just the teeniest bit resentful. Has he decided I'm a difficult patient? So, he says, looking down at his hands, So what's the score at the moment? What method are you using now?

I must think about this. I can't say French letter to *him*. But the official words, the words I know I ought to use, stick in the throat. My husband is taking precautions, I say. Mr Gamble writes down Sheath, and asks if it's satisfactory for us, me and my husband.

Pictures float into my head; my husband groping in his bedside drawer, having knocked the lamp over; me lying in the dark with nothing to do and going off the boil, if I was ever on it; our children wandering round our bedroom before breakfast while I'm getting dressed or putting my face on, touching things, picking up

30

things, opening drawers. What are these, Mum? What are they *for*? Not just pictures. Some man once told me that doing it in a French letter is like sucking a sweet with the wrapper on.

It's not ideal, I say to Mr G.

No, it's not. Mr G. says. It's not much fun for your husband, I can promise you that. Even more important, perhaps, it's not really *safe*. The accident rate is high. Have the two of you ever considered – he pauses, he presses the tips of his fingers together, and then pushes them apart – sterilization? A vasectomy? I tell him we have, but one of us might, you never know, die of a heart attack or get run over by a bus, and the other might then remarry someone who hadn't had children and who wanted some.

Mr G. glances at his watch. Let's re-cap, he says. Which method you've tried was, d'you think, if not entirely satisfactory, then on balance the best for you, the best for both of you? Remembering, of course, that no method – apart from sterilization, and we've ruled that out – is a hundred per cent?

The Coil, I say. Because it has to be the Coil. At least with the Coil you know it's there, and you don't have to remember to swallow anything; or coat something with sperm-killing cream and stick it up yourself. And remember to take it out afterwards (but not too soon, not before the sperm-killers have had a chance to be effective), and wash it and dry it and dust it with talcum powder; and not leave it on the basin when the telephone rings.

Mr Gamble, looking at me, opens a drawer in his desk and places what he finds there on the surface between us. He pushes at it with his forefinger. This is the Copper Coil, he says, triumphantly, like a conjuror at the end of a difficult trick, and I think we should give it a try.

The Copper Coil is very small. It is not shaped like a coil; it is a piece of bent fusewire; half a hairpin; a shorthand character; a rest in music. How could it possibly prevent a baby?

We're not exactly sure, Mr G. admits, still pushing the wire around with his finger, but we know it does. Of course there's bound to be some failure rate, but it's a low one as these things go.

31

I'd like to try it for at least three months, to give it a chance to settle down, and then if you aren't happy with it, or have problems of any kind, we've still got the low-dose Pill to fall back on. The side effects have been minimized since you last tried it. Failing that, a Diaphragm in conjunction with a sperm-killing gel. Right then – Mr G. leans back in his chair and pushes at the desk as though he's trying to get rid of it – I think we'd better have a little peep at you. If you'd like to pop up on the day bed over there. Just remove your tights and pants and bra, but keep your slip on if you're wearing one.

We get up together. My skirt is sticking to my bottom and to the backs of my knees. Am I supposed to take my bag with me, or leave it on the floor by my chair? I walked to the curtained-off corner where the day bed waits, Mr G. to the cabinet where, presumably, his disposable gloves and his instruments are.

It's dark behind the curtain. I take off my shirt, my skirt, my shoes, my tights, my pants. With difficulty and without removing my petticoat – for although it's a hot day I am wearing one, I knew I should need it – I unhook my bra. I fold all these things on a chair, covering my underclothes with my outer clothes. I clamber onto the day bed, which is high. It has a hard flat pillow and draw sheet, across which has been laid a square of linen the size of a baby's cot sheet. Am I meant to lie on top of this, or under it? I lie under it, or rather arrange it to cover as much of my lower half as it will. My feet are turned out; my heels are resting on a length of cellophane that crackles when I move them.

A light snaps on above me. The curtains rattle back. It's Mr G. who does this. He is just going to examine my breasts, he says, he is sorry if his hands are cold, he's washed them, can I slip my shoulder straps down for him please!

If people can be divided into those who look better, and more themselves, naked, and those who look better, and more themselves, wearing clothes, I must come into the second category. My mammary glands, in particular, don't stand up to scrutiny. They aren't, alas they never were, composed of two firm

and perfectly moulded hillocks from which twin rosy budlets
spring. They fall, when I lie on my back, flatly away from the
breastbone and sag either side of the ribcage like two badly-filled
shopping bags. An exaggeration? My bosom is a sad sight; if I
allow myself to think about it, I weep; if I glimpse it in the
bathroom glass, I turn my back. Were it not that my husband
professes, once every five years, to be fond of my bosom, I should
have cut my throat long ago.

I stare at the ceiling and tell myself he has seen worse sights than
this, while, with the flat of his hands, Mr Gamble goes over the
part of me I've just described. Do you do this at home? he asks, as
he squeezes, prods and cups. You should, you know, at least once a
month, in front of the mirror. That's fine, he says (How does he
know it's fine? How, with all these lumps and bumps, could he
tell if any of them were unusual?) He pulls the cot sheet up over my
top half, so that my lower half is now exposed. He presses the folds
of my stomach, he pushes his fingers in hard at the sides, just above
the groin. Any tenderness here? Or here? Relax. Let yourself go
limp. Now, now I'd like you to roll over onto your side and draw
your knees up for me as high as you can.

I roll over on my side to the wall and draw my knees up, just a
little. Higher, if you can, Mr G. says. He tucks my petticoat out of
the way; he tweaks the cot sheet from my shoulders and removes it
altogether. I grip the edge of the mattress. I screw my eyes tight
shut– for by doing so I may be able to blot from my imagination
the terrible view Mr G. now has of me: the spots on my bottom I
tried to disguise with talcum powder before I set out; the
corrugated skin in the groove below my coccyx; the –

Try not to tense yourself, Mr G. says, as his gloved hands part
me. One of these hands, the left hand, stays on my left *buttock*; the
other hand, the right hand, bypasses my (now what would he call
it? *Anus*? *The opening of the alimentary canal*?) bum hole; enters
somewhere below this. Excavates. Explores. Probes. La la la, I sing
to myself, la la la, to shut out the sound (of old men drinking soup,
of gumboots being pulled from a bog) that accompanies the

33

withdrawal of this hand. La la la la la.

You may feel this a little, Mr G. says. No, don't tense, let yourself go. La la la la, pom, pom, pom, pom, let yourself go, I sing to myself, as the plunger, or whatever it is, twists in deeper and deeper, to my very core, centre, kernel, essence, nucleus, thesaurus. *Thesaurus?* Or thes*aurus?* Which should it be? If in danger, cross your legs; if you can't be good be careful; if sex is inevitable, relax and enjoy it; if –

All done, all finished, Mr G. says, you can get dressed again now.

I suppose I'll bleed a bit, I say to Mr G. when I am dressed again and back in my chair. (I'm an old hand at this; I seem to remember a bloody aftermath to Coil insertions.)

I see no reason for that, Mr G. says. He looks puzzled. Oh I see – I should have made myself clearer. What you've had was merely a routine smear test, long overdue. If all's in order in that department, you'll get an appointment card from the Infirmary. Until very recently, he confides, I did Coil insertions here, in the Consulting Rooms, but it's safer and more hygienic in Theatre, where everything's to hand. It's better for the patient. More comfortable.

I've never had it done in a hospital before, I say. (I'm not at all sure.) I'm not sure –

There's absolutely nothing to worry about, believe me – Mr G. stretches a pinstriped arm across the desk and pats my hand – Feeling all right now, dear?

We get up. Mr G. walks with me to the door, one arm lightly around my shoulder. There's nothing sinister about this, I'm certain. I'm quite sure this is the way he dismisses all his patients.

*

And now it is evening, our children tucked in their beds, what's left of the fish pie back in the larder. My husband is sitting in an armchair, reading a book. I am sitting in an identical chair, cobbling a seam in a pair of my son's jeans. There was no blue cotton in the sewing box, so I am making do with green.

I went to see the gynae today, I say to my husband.

My husband turns two pages at once of his book, Alan Moorehead's *Gallipoli.* He has read it before, a long time ago, but is looking something up.

What? Oh yes. How did it go? Is he a good egg, d'you think, your Mr Whatsisname?

I don't know. I think he may be. He took a lot of trouble (for it's true; he did take a lot of trouble). His name is Gamble.

Ho ho, my husband says, going back to the index. You'd think he'd change it. He runs his finger down the page. Can't seem to find it, damn, he says.

He's giving me another Coil, I say. I've got to have it done in the Infirmary.

Why's that? What for? my husband asks, his eye still on the index. What does that mean exactly? *In nuce*, mind you, not *verbatim*, says my husband who is a Latin tag man, a man for whom all invoices are, *per se* and *ipso facto,* (if *a priori*) *pro forma*, all payments *ex gratia*, all evidence *prima facie*, all quids *pro quo.*

It's safer and more hygienic in hospital, in Theatre, Mr Gamble says.

That makes sense, my husband murmurs to the index, that makes sense.

I'm not too keen on the idea of Theatre, I say. I'd rather have it done in the Consulting Rooms, or the Clinic, like last time.

Don't then, my husband says. He takes off his spectacles and puts them back on again. You're the customer, I'm paying for this, remember. Do what you want to do. Have it done where you want.

But Mr Gamble doesn't do it in the Consulting Rooms any more. He said –

You told me what he said, and it makes sense to me, my husband says. He clearly has a *causa movens.* Stop worrying, he says, *nil desperandum.*

There is silence for a while. My husband leaves the room and returns with the whisky bottle, which is nearly empty. We must have clobbered it before supper, he says.

I had to have an internal examination today, I tell him.

I'm sure you did, my husband says. He sips his whisky. Poor you, he says, how horrid for you, poor you.

When we were newly married my husband came with me on my first visit to a gynaecologist. I wasn't sure I wanted him as a matter of fact, but he insisted. He was very distressed. I cannot bear the idea of another man touching you, even looking at you, he said as we drew up outside the surgery. I cannot bear it, you are mine – and he thumped the steering wheel in despair. When I came out an hour later I found him hunched in the driving seat, and when I got in beside him he clung to me. My baby, he said, his eyes full of tears, my precious, precious baby. I imagine that my husband, who is a positive, forward-looking man and, Latin tags and military campaigns apart, never one to dwell on the past, has long since forgotten this incident.

I bite off the end of my cotton and take another item from the mending pile at my feet. Emerald green will not do for the rip in Angelica's scarlet party dress, but there's a reel of crimson Sylko in my lap which will have to.

*

The queue in Reception is very long, and I join the end of it. I'm annoyed by this queue because it wasn't easy getting here on time. I had to organize, which means beg, someone else to do the school run; we had to have breakfast before seven; I had to drive my husband to the station, get back, make sandwiches for two school lunch boxes, put the dustbins out, and then walk the dogs – because who knows how long they're going to be shut up for. All this so I could leave the house by ten to eight, so I could be here by half past.

There's a telephone on the Reception desk. It rings and rings. It rings all the time I'm waiting, all the time I'm inching up the queue. No less than three people to deal with appointments and enquiries, and yet none of them can answer this telephone. None of them so much as looks at it, and it's odd. I know I couldn't work at a desk where a telephone was ringing without doing something about it, without at least taking it off the hook, or shouting at it.

Follow the sign to B2, the Receptionist says when I hand her my card, and she jerks her head to her right. Your telephone is ringing, by the way, I tell her. Card please, she says to the person next in line.

I follow the signs to B2. Left from the desk through swing doors, right at the end of the corridor, up two levels in the lift, more swing doors, B2. A nurse is heading towards me. She's going fast, and when I accost her she has to brake, so that her black shoes squeak on the lino. I tell her my name and what I'm here for, and she turns back the way she's come and points to a door on the right. Go in there, she says, take off your clothes and put on a theatre gown and a dressing-gown, and I'll be back in a jiff.

In the room there's a cupboard, partitioned down the middle: theatre gowns on the left, dressing-gowns on the right. I take off my clothes and put on a theatre gown. It is like a high-necked apron with sleeves, and it fastens at the back with tapes, one of which is missing. I bend my head into the cupboard and sniff the dressing-gowns to see if they've been worn, but they smell of nothing. I put one on. It is voluminous. Its sleeves come down over my hands, its skirts trail over the floor. I hitch it at the waist, and blouse and bag it over the tie-belt. I don't like these clothes, and the nothing smell of them. I want to pee. I want to go home.

I sit on the bed and swing my legs and wait for the nurse. She doesn't come. I've got time to consider what I don't want to consider, the question I meant to ask, and didn't ask, Mr Gamble, the problem I meant to discuss, and didn't discuss, with my husband, namely this: Is it all right to have a Coil? Is it all right to put a foreign body, a *piece of wire* (even if copper wire) in the womb? Does the womb like it? Is it dangerous in any way? To the womb? To me in general? Last time, and the time before, I bled

37

like a, like a *stuck pig*. I was a social embarrassment. I had to leave
dinner parties in a hurry. I mean, is it okay to have a Coil? Is the
Coil an okay thing to have?

I get off the bed and shuffle to the window. Far below two tiny
figures in navy capes are being blown along a concrete walkway.
They weave in and out of the buildings, disappear, reappear beside
a grove of sapling poplars, vanish into Pathology, a shack like all
the other shacks. Angelica's classroom is a shack. She will be in it
now – arithmetic, first period after prayers. She didn't want to go
to school today. She didn't feel well, she said. She had a headache
and a tummy ache, she felt *sick*. She says this, or something like it,
every morning. Every morning I want to keep her at home and let
her mess up the kitchen table with paintwater and scissors and
gummed squares; every morning I send her to school.

I go out into the corridor. There's a cleaner with a hovercraft
outside my door. She shows me where the lavatory is, just in time.

I am back on the bed, curled up, reading the mail that came as I
was leaving the house. My mail is one postcard, from a friend
who's on holiday in Kenya (was on holiday, I should say. I saw her
in Tescos yesterday, at the cheese counter. She was busy, I was
busy, we pretended not to see each other). The card is addressed to
Memsahib Pomfrey. It says Jambo! Habari? We are having a
fantastic time. See you soonest, Love V & C. I turn it over. The
picture side has a hippo with its mouth open, half submerged in a
pool, surrounded by smaller hippos.

A man's head appears round the door of my room. I've come to
take you to Theatre, he says. Leave your handbag and your clothes
in the locker – and your watch if you're wearing one.

Are you a nurse? I ask the man when we are in the lift together,
descending to G level. The man has his arms folded across his chest
and is staring at the ceiling the way people tend to in lifts. I know I
do, because it's the only way to avoid eyeball to eyeball
confrontation with strangers. He uncrosses his arms and points to
a badge on his overall which says Porter, green letters on white.

At G Level we follow signs to X-Ray and Haematology, but at

38

the last moment bypass these and make now for Pharmacy, Out-patients Surgical, Gynaecology and Shop. We walk out through plastic swing doors, Emergency Exit 2, and I lift my skirts, costume drama style, onto covered concrete, uncovered concrete, covered concrete, through swing doors, into lino corridor, where we stop. Put on a pair of overshoes, the porter says, and take a seat here.

Against the wall are two chairs and a row of see-through galoshes, all the same size; it doesn't matter which pair I choose. I take a seat in the corridor. On my left are the shut double doors of Theatre 1 and Theatre 2, and opposite to me on the wall is a notice in red: This is a No Smoking Zone. I look from the notice to the doors and back again. Zone. It's an odd word; the longer I stare at it, the odder it is. Zone. *Zone*. What does it mean? Does it mean anything? No. No such number, no such zone. (This time I'm gonna take it myself, and put it right in her hand, and if it comes back the vurry next day, *then* I'll understand the writing on it) –

The doors of Theatre 2 open, a stretcher trolley shoots out, swings round, one person behind it pushing, another in front steering, holding the drip steady. I keep my head down as they trundle past at a trot, but I see because I want to see, because I have to, because I must: a white face, a dead face, surely, chin tipped up, mouth hugely open, a tube in the nose – or was it the mouth? Gone.

How long have I been here? Ten minutes? Twenty? I keep checking, but on my left wrist, printed across unbleached hairs and a mole, is only the ghost of my watch. Where is Mr G.? Why doesn't Mr G. come?

Ready for you in theatre now, dear.

It isn't Mr G., it's a nurse, in green, masked and gowned, who leads me, clopping in my overshoes, out of the darkness of the corridor into the light of Theatre 1.

It is very bright in Theatre. Interval time. The house lights are up and there's a party going on. It's a tea party, I can tell, because the six or seven people wandering about chatting have cups and saucers in their hands. It's surprising really, all this activity and chat and tea drinking, because you tend to think of hospital theatres as sterile, hygienic places, as Mr G. said, places (or areas, or *zones*) you can only enter if you're wearing overshoes.

Someone comes forward and helps me out of my dressing-gown. Someone asks me to take off my overshoes and my shoes. This same person gives me a hand onto the stage. (No, not a stage, a table. An operating table, for operations.) I lie down on my back, feet together, arms by my sides. Lift your tail, please. And at once, when I comply, the theatre gown is rolled back, up over my knees and thighs, and then folded above my waist. My legs are separated into a V. My right leg is carried up and away and placed in a sling and strapped; my left leg is carried up and away and placed in a sling and strapped. I raise my head. The slings are attached to a contraption suspended from the ceiling. It's like a Big Top up there: lights, wires, machinery, all the gear for tightropes and trapeze.

My bottom, my *tail*, is no longer on the table. Somebody slips a pillow underneath me, wedges it into the small of my back.

And that's all. Nothing else happens. I am on my back, with no knickers on, my legs wide apart and in the air – and nothing happens. The tea party is still going on, to be sure, all round me I can hear chatter and laughter and cups being returned to saucers – but I'm not part of it somehow, no one offers me a cup, no one chats to me.

This is not the first time I've been in this position; our second daughter, in no hurry to be born, had to be induced. But that time there were only two people in the Treatment Room – me, and the hospital doctor (Brown? Yes, Brown) who explained nothing, who said nothing, as he strapped up my legs. I remember the pain when he *ruptured the membranes;* I remember thinking it must be blood that gushed out and ran back underneath me and soaked the hospital gown and the sheets; I remember the ward sister in the corridor who, as I staggered out into it, took one look and snapped her fingers: Nurse! That girl needs some pethadine! I can think of all this, and concentrate on the detail and the pain because nothing that happens today, nothing that Mr G. has got up his sleeve, can be as bad as that.

Or can it? At least last time there was an end-product, a baby, Michael, to be born, at least there was someone to look forward to. What Mr G. is going to do (why doesn't he do it?) is prevent a baby being born; and at the same time rob me (when I am tired or cross, or simply not in the mood for love) of the best, the most convincing, the least hurtful, of my nocturnal excuses: D'you think we should, darling, when we know it isn't *safe*?

There's a game I used to play with my brothers, that I daresay everyone plays with their brothers – or sisters – if they have them: the Would You Rather Game. Would you rather be (here describe the worst horror you are capable of inventing) or go to bed with (here name the most repellent specimen, of either sex, known to you all). Would you rather be on your back under a search light with your legs apart and no knickers on in the middle of a tea party, or . . .

All right, Mrs Pomfrey, dear? I'm afraid you will feel this, it will be a bit painful. But if you can relax and just allow yourself to go floppy, it will make it easier for you. It's Mr G.'s voice. It's Mr G.'s face, bending over mine, I recognize his eyes. He has pulled his mask down, below his chin, so that he can speak to me. I can see the bristles on his top lip and the hairs, wonderfully luxuriant hairs, in his nose. Has he been here all the time?

There is less chatter now, no chinking of cups. But no one has left the Theatre; I'm certain of this because if I roll my head to the right I can see the doors, and even if I couldn't see, even if I were blind, I'd feel the draught. Mr G. prepares to insert the Coil. While he does so, he gives a commentary, an *ex tempore* lecture, my husband would say, to the throng at the end of the table because, yes, that is where the tea party is now assembled. They are students, of course they are! And I am the demonstration model. Watch closely, Mr G. says, I'm just going to lubricate the vagina prior to insertion. Can you tell us about the relative safety and efficiency of this Coil? a male voice, eager beaver, enquires. How does this Coil, the copper Coil, compare with other Inter-uterine devices currently available?

All over, Mr G. says at last, all done. Good girl.

My legs are unstrapped, removed from their slings and returned to me. I am helped down from the table. An S2, please, Mr G. says, and someone springs forward with a cellophane packet which, snipped open, contains two sanitary towels, individually and hygienically wrapped. You will have a period now, Mr G. promises, placing one of the sanitary towels between my thighs, but if the loss is unduly heavy don't hesitate to give us a ring. Take two aspirin four-hourly if there's any discomfort.

Dressing-gown on, shoes on, overshoes on. Out of theatre. A six-yard stumble on cardboard legs. Overshoes off. And here is the porter, come to take me back to my clothes.

There are some questions I forgot to ask Mr G. and the tea party in Theatre 1. How do you hold a sanitary towel in place when you haven't been given a belt or a pair of pants? How do you keep up with a porter in a hurry when your legs refuse to function properly, and when you're trying to glue your thighs together so that your ST won't leak or land on the floor? When your dressing-gown was designed for a giant and is intent on tripping you up? When your insides are falling out, when your eyes are blurred and you can't see where you're going, when the pain is so bad you will surely faint, if not actually die?

In the lift, ascending to B2, a trickle – hot, sticky, but which cannot be amniotic fluid, not today – descends the inside of my right thigh, circumnavigates the knee muscle, finds a route down the calf, steers between the ankle and heel, arrives in my shoe, collects there.

Outside my door the porter and I part company. Here we are then, he says, the first words he's spoken since we left the theatre, and he goes. I reach out for the door handle of sanctuary, and then I notice it, a red-black splash on the beige lino at my feet, the size of a coin, a little ragged around the edge. I turn, and look, there are more of them, all down the corridor back the way we've come, dark two-penny pieces, regularly spaced, as far as the eye can see. I've left a trail, like Hansel and Gretel did in the forest! Supposing, just supposing, I wanted to go back to Theatre now, I wouldn't need a porter to show me the way.

*

Afterword 1: The Letters
Unposted letter to Mr Gamble.

Dear Mr Gamble,
   A week after my experience in the Infirmary I wrote you a letter.
   I decided to write to you for two reasons: a) because I felt you should know what it was like to be on the receiving end of your lack of attention, and b) because I thought it incumbent on me, being articulate, to suggest ways of improving your set-up.
   I took trouble over my letter. The first two drafts were too emotional (you mustn't be allowed to excuse yourself on the grounds that you were dealing with an hysteric); the third too rude. In the end my letter was polite, neither sarcastic nor acrimonious. I gave you a matter-of-fact account of what happened to me. I said I thought you'd want to know about it, so that the experience couldn't be repeated for anyone else. I suggested a few things (a female nurse to take the patient to and from Theatre; fewer people, if possible, present in Theatre; the provision of a sanitary belt or pants afterwards) to make it less of an ordeal for other women in future. Yours sincerely, etc., etc.
   Nineteen days later I got your reply: seven typewritten lines, sincerely regretting 'the problems you encountered in the Day Case Unit', hoping the Coil was 'proving satisfactory' – signed in your absence by your secretary, and enclosing your bill.
   Could you please tell me, because it wasn't quite clear, which part of the Infirmary was the Day Case Unit?

Afterword 2: The Titles

I had difficulty deciding on a title for this story. I hope I chose the right one (the right one, that is, for the story, and also for you). It cannot be said to mislead, although it may be on the dull side. If you did find it dull, you might be interested to see, in case there's one here you prefer, the other titles I rejected in favour of it. Before I list them, I'd like to tell you my reason for discarding them. It's that, when I typed them out, I saw they could all be construed as containing bitter little ironies; they all seemed to smack of, if not quite feminist, womens' or alternative writing.

I was worried they might, if you're a man, put you off.

Here they are, then, in order of invention, not merit:

1) The Would You Rather Game
2) That's Enough Gynaecology – Ed.
3) *Volenti Non Fit Injuria**
4) How to Make Your Man Happy in Bed.

*Which is what Lettice's husband said, not unsympathetically and among other things, when she told him what happened in Theatre. It seemed quite neat for a while, perhaps the best of the bunch, I nearly settled for it; but not everyone appreciates Latin tags, some people consider them a joke or pretentious, not everyone understands them.

Mad About The Boy

He got her through school which she hated. On Saturdays, and on weekday evenings after prep, they were allowed to play the gramophone. She would take hers, a German machine in a blue-black leather case her father had found in Berlin at the end of the war, into a corner of the gym and set herself up. The inside of the gramophone had an intoxicating smell. Each time she lifted the lid she sniffed hard. Years later, searching a junk shop for something to stand plants on, she came across an old gramophone and opened it up and sniffed and was immediately taken back; she could see that German machine: the catches on the case that released the lid, the heavy head tucked safely to the side, the winder secured by two brackets inside the lid, the sliding compartment for needles, the needles themselves in their shiny tin boxes.

She was nine or ten when the passion started and her collection of his records amounted to less than a dozen. She had stolen them from her mother and her aunts. All, with the exception of 'Don't Let's be Beastly to the Germans', were pre-war and recorded before she was born. Three were twelve-inch and scenes from plays *(Private Lives; Cavalcade; Tonight at 8.30)*. The rest were ten-inch and songs, sung solo by Noel with a piano accompaniment. Sometimes she listened in silence, kneeling close against the gramophone with her head inside the lid so as not to miss a syllable; more often she sang along with him in a clipped tenor as near his own as she could manage. Soon she was spending all her pocket money on records: 'Don't Make Fun of the Festival'; 'There are Bad Times Just Around the Corner'; 'Matelot'. His voice in these seemed rounder – or was it thicker? – which fitted in with his being almost bald now and not as thin as he'd been in the photographs she owned of *Private Lives*.

Noel's popularity was at a low ebb in the early nineteen fifties, a fact she discovered from the gossip columns of the daily newspapers. He seemed to be in trouble with the press for living most of the time in Bermuda or Jamaica and thereby avoiding income tax, and he was having a rough time with the critics for writing plays which, they were all agreed, showed none of his pre-war brilliance. He was not popular at her school, Belmont, but that was because most people had never heard of him, the few that had knowing him only as a vague figure – like Fred Astaire or Jack Buchanan – from their parents' youth. The decline in his fortunes suited her very well and made her feel protective. She alone really appreciated him. She alone understood him and his problems. She alone knew, and sympathized with, the weaknesses of his literary style. These included an over-fondness for adjectives and an inability to resist, in his plays, the witty line even when it was at odds with the character who had to speak it.

By the time she was twelve she knew, she was sure, everything there was to know about him; not just about the plays – date, theatre, cast, length of run were all at her fingertips – but his private life and his character. He was kind and sentimental and generous and hardworking, someone who never put off till the afternoon what he could do in the morning. He did not suffer fools. He was of course clever, but perhaps not in an intellectual way. He was witty and funny. He had no false modesty about his talents. He was not a believer, except in himself, and this was bothering because God might strike him down. She was keen on God and often spent as much as an hour on her knees on the splintery boards of Burne-Jones (the dormitories were named after painters) before getting into bed. She had once heard Colonel Symes, an acquaintance of her father's, refer to Noel as 'that old pansy'. This, so far as she could gather, meant that he preferred men to women in some respects. If he did, it didn't bother her. It was so obvious that he liked women and that he loved them too. He was always loyal about the women he loved. She knew who they were: his mother and G. E. Calthrop (Gladys) and Lorn Loraine and Joyce Carey. And Gertrude Lawrence. She loved Gertie almost as much as she loved Noel and kept a scrap book for each of them into which she pasted newspaper cuttings, theatre programmes and notices.

In the school holidays she haunted the second-hand bookshop in the market town where her mother did most of her shopping. The shop, Burkes, had high ceilings and the bookshelves went right up to them. There were books everywhere, not just on the shelves but in untidy stacks on the floor and in parked trolleys that blocked the aisles. A rickety staircase led to more books upstairs, but she seldom climbed them because the theatre section was on the ground floor. The shop, poorly lit and with alleyways that turned corners and resembled streets, made her think of a town at dusk.

Among her finds at Burkes was a brown book with a battered spine entitled *The Amazing Mr. Noel Coward* by Patrick Braybrooke. The book, in itself disappointing, had been made special by its previous owner who'd stuck photographs and press cuttings on all the available space of the end-papers. There was a caricature of Noel and Gertie taken from *The New Yorker*, a newspaper clip of Noel and Beatrice Lillie dining 'intimately' at a restaurant, and another cutting, so large it had had to be folded over, the caption of which read: 'At Goldenhurst Farm: Gertrude Lawrence, Noel Coward and Jack Wilson his Business Partner'. The photograph showed a tea party on a lawn. Gertie, sitting up very straight, poured out from a silver tea pot while a huge dog, a setter possibly, leaned across the table and licked her nose. Noel lay in a wicker chair, which was old-fashioned and had a wheel at the back. One of his knees was bent up. He held a saucer in his left hand and a cup in his right which partly obscured his face, and he eyed Gertie over the rim. The business partner who sat astride another wicker chair which did not have a wheel, was reading a magazine. Behind him a bag of golf clubs posed against a brick pillar. The domesticity of the scene was thrilling, although Goldenhurst – from the photograph all diamond panes and beams – was not to her taste.

Reading Noel was not easy to do at Belmont, where books brought back by the girls had to be passed as suitable by the headmistress, Miss Church. You put your books on an oak chest outside her drawing-room door and at some time, probably in the middle of the night for no one ever saw them go, they were taken inside. If they passed, they reappeared two days later in the same miraculous fashion, and you were then free to remove them and read them. She'd put *Fallen Angels* and *The Vortex* out once but had not seen them again until the end of term, when they were handed to her with a wan smile. After that she smuggled his plays in and kept them under a packet of sanitary towels in her underclothes drawer. She learned them, in bed and with a torch, after lights out.

Before falling asleep she invented a 'dream' about him. The dream was always the same. On a foggy afternoon she would escape down the drive (pitted tarmac and enclosed by species rhododendrons and ponticums, now glistening unpleasantly in the fog) and walk the two miles to the station and the London train. At Waterloo she'd take a taxi to 17 Gerald Road, the studio flat he lived in when he wasn't in Jamaica or wherever. He came to the door himself, peered down, saw at a glance how fascinating she was under her cloak of shyness, and invited her in for tea. Tea was crumpets in a silver dish, accompanied by light and witty conversation. She made him laugh a lot. After tea he showed her his treasures and his books and pictures (these included two landscapes he'd painted himself) until they were interrupted by actor friends dropping in for cocktails. He was proprietorial about her and introduced her to them with pride, as though he himself had invented her. Occasionally he'd pat her head, which made her blush with pleasure. When his visitors were invited to stay on for supper she stayed too and helped Cole (she knew about Cole from reading *Present Indicative*) serve it. They had cold roast mutton and baked potatoes and onion sauce and salad, followed by apple pie and cheese and biscuits. There was red wine to drink.

Coffee was served in the drawing-room. Noel ('Do stop calling me Mr. Coward, there's a darling') sat down at the grand piano and played a few bars. 'Antonia!' – he beckoned her with a finger – 'Come and sing a duet with me.' They sang 'You Were There' from *Shadow Play*. She owned the record of this, and had sung Gertie's part so often, copying every idiosyncratic note, that she sounded just like her, she thought. Noel seemed to think so too. Eventually the visitors began to drift away, fetching sable wraps – the women – and capes and white silk scarves – the men – from Noel's bedroom. When she said 'I must go now,' he said 'Not in this fog dear, and in any case you've missed the last train.' So she stayed. Dressed in a pair of his pyjamas – they were slub silk and striped in pink and grey – she slept, curled up beside him in his huge double bed under a black satin quilt with scarlet roses on it.

At home she was teased about her passion, but not unkindly. Her mother – 'I was a Coward fan long before you were born' – quite liked him, and her sister Fran, who was eighteen, liked him very much. Fran's teasing often took the form of trying to trip her up on dialogue from the plays. They might be sitting at lunch when Fran would suddenly stare out of the window and point and say: 'That hedge over there is called Cupressus Macrocapa,' to which the only possible reply (there were no hedges of the sort in their garden) was: 'Do you swear it?' Or again, she might be minding her own business in an arm chair with a book, when Fran would materialize at her side and ask: 'Are you engaged for this dance?' The correct answer, which of course she always gave, being: 'I was, but I'll cut it if you promise to love me always and never let anyone or anything come between us, ever.' Her father addressed her, and often in the third person, as Lady Coward, even though Noel at the time was plain Mr. 'Some more roast beef for Lady C.?' – he would turn from the sideboard with his carving knife and his eyebrows raised. Or 'Lady Coward is in a pretty bloody mood today, it seems.' Asked for something for her autograph book, he wrote unkindly on one page: *Nobody loves a fat girl/Nobody gives me a date/The only game I play with the boys/Is sitting and guessing my weight*, and on the facing one, right in the middle: *I am a Nole and I live in a hole*. He drew a picture of the hole, and beside it a signpost on which he printed: *Montego Bay 3 miles*.

One day, feeling fat and bored and sad, she looked Noel up in the A-D volume of the London Telephone Directory, not expecting to find him there. Yet there he was, his name in ordinary print like everyone else's and there was his telephone number: SLOane 2965. For three days she did nothing except chant the number. Say she got through and managed to speak to him? A furious: 'Who are you? What do you want? Go away, please.' Click – the likely outcome – would put paid to her fantasy for ever. So she compromised. The compromise consisted of asking the operator for SLOane 2965 and then sweating with fear while the number was obtained. When it was engaged, which was often, the anti-climax was balanced by a dull relief. Whenever the operator said: It's ringing now, caller,' she felt sick with terror and replaced her receiver as soon as his was lifted. Sitting in her father's chair in the empty drawing-room, she would shake and speculate: Who had lifted the receiver? Was it him? Or Cole? A maid? A friend? A lover? The thrill lay in the knowledge that she had caused a bell to ring in his house and that if he were in he must surely hear it. If only in the minutest way she had affected his life. Because of something she had done he had perhaps called out: 'Answer that, Coley, would you?' or 'Who the hell's that? Tell them I'm not in'. Or, if Coley and maids and cooks and friends and lovers were absent, he himself might have padded – in his dressing-gown? – to the telephone and picked up the receiver with his own hands. The possibilities were endless.

As with a drug, the telephone episodes satisfied for a time and produced highs and lows. Soon a stronger dose was needed. So that when her best friend from school with whom she sometimes stayed in the holidays, dared her to speak to him, she decided to take on the dare. They did it from a telephone box outside the Post Office and Stores in the Suffolk village where Christina lived. There was a good deal of preliminary giggling and pinching – Christina carried on like that much of the time in any case – and scrabbling on the filthy floor of the call box for the pennies they kept dropping. Eventually the operator said: 'You're through now, caller', and after a pause and some clicks, a male voice that was not his said: 'SLOane 2965.' 'Hello', she said. 'Could I speak to Mr. Coward please?' 'He's at the theatre at the moment, I'm afraid'. The voice sounded wary (but it could have been true, she decided afterwards. He was playing King Magnus in *The Apple Cart* that summer). 'Can I take a message?' 'My name is Amanda Prynne,' she spoke very fast, turning her back on Christina who was bent up with laughter and clutching her stomach. 'Isn't that a coincidence?' 'It certainly is,' the voice said politely, disbelievingly. 'I can't wait. I can't, I can't' Christina had started to wail. 'I'm going to do it NOW.' She wasn't sure what to say next to the voice on the telephone. Instead, it spoke to her: 'Mr Coward will be most interested to hear about you. Thank you for calling. Goodbye.' 'Wait!' she shouted, but the line had gone dead. Christina uncrossed her skinny legs and unleased a stream of pee that struck the floor of the box as a waterfall strikes rocks, splashing their bare legs and soaking their sandals. They quarrelled all the way home to the Regency rectory where Christina lived, but by the time they reached the bathroom and were unpeeling their smelly clothes they were giggling again. 'What did he say? What did he say?' Christina aimed a loaded sponge at her and missed. 'Who's this Amanda person, anyway?'

The following day she shut herself in the lavatory, and took up her pen: 'Dear Mr. Coward, As you may have heard, I telephoned you yesterday . . . ' She covered two whole sides. She told him how much she admired him and how she knew everything he'd ever written. She said she hoped he didn't mind her writing to him. She signed herself Amanda Prynne. The letter was written on Christina's mother's headed paper: Bumpstead Hall, nr Haverhill,

Suffolk, which she hoped would impress him. Leaning out of the carriage window as her train pulled out of Audley End station, she asked Christina, as casually as she could, to forward any letters that came for Amanda Prynne.

Silence is ambiguous stuff, she discovered. Almost anything could be read into it. Sometimes he opened her letter, scanned its contents briefly, crumpled it and dropped it in a wastepaper basket. Sometimes (he did this more often) he read her letter carefully and with increasing interest, then sat down at his desk, unscrewed his Parker 51, filled it with Quink and wrote a reply. It was a kind note, quite short, and it ended with an invitation (to tea, but she knew where *that* would lead). When the weeks that went by became months and she could no longer believe in his letter, she allowed herself to think that he didn't want to spoil things by writing, but that he kept hers on his bedside table, tucked inside a favourite book – *Barchester Towers*, perhaps. She knew everything about him. She knew of his addiction to Trollope.

It was about this time that something happened to bring the real world and the fantasy world briefly if electrifyingly closer. Copies of *The Times,* the only newspaper considered suitable reading for the girls at Belmont, were kept in a Jacobean oak cradle in the hall, disproportionately large and imposing for the house which had been built at the turn of the century in baronial style for, rumour had it, a Spanish ambassador who for some reason had never arrived. The floor of the hall was on two levels, the lower level, nearest the front door, being paved with large black and white stone squares and empty except for an enormous J. Arthur Rank gong struck at mealtimes by Brooks the butler whom everybody hated; the higher level oak-boarded and part-covered by an ancient (that was easy to believe: it was almost threadbare) and, so they were always being told, priceless, Persian carpet no one was allowed to tread on. No one, that is, except for Miss Church. The cradle was on the higher level, and beside it was an oak chest you sat on if you wanted to read the paper (it was forbidden to remove *The Times* from the hall). She was seated there one morning at break,kicking her heels against the chest and giving the personal columns on the front page her usual close attention, when a small paragraph winked at her like a neon sign: 'Mr. Noel Coward will be at the Times Bookshop at noon tomorrow (Tuesday) to sign copies of *The Noel Coward Song Book*.'

There was no chance of escaping in fog (it was in any case July) on the London train. She'd spent her pocket money for the term and had nothing for the fare. She did not know where the Times Bookshop was. She tore a page from her rough notebook (it was forbidden to tear pages from your rough notebook) and wrote to Fran who was doing a secretarial course in Bayswater and who lived with three friends in a basement flat off Royal Avenue:

Darling Fran,
Noel Coward is signing copies of the N.C. Song Book TOMORROW (Tues.) at the Times Bookshop. Please get one for me in yr lunch hour. I swear I will repay. I'm sorry to be such a nuisance. Please please PLEASE!
T.O.L.
Ant.

She gave her letter to the under-matron, Miss Tankland, who shopped in the town on Monday afternoons. Miss Tankland did not like her any more than she, or any other of the girls, liked Miss Tankland, who was spiteful, two-faced, a snob and stupid (she had once said to Camilla Arbuthnot: 'I believe you're quite well connected' and had not perceived the irony in Camilla's reply: 'Yes. The ninth earl died last week'). It was quite on the cards that Tank would lose her letter on purpose.

The next day was a day of suffering. Would Fran get her letter – always supposing Tank had posted it – before she left for Bayswater? If she did get it, would she act on it? She had a feeling she hadn't told Fran what time Noel was supposed to be at the shop.

After tea, which as usual had been buns and compo strawberry jam out of a tin with woodshavings added for pips, she was searching her desk for Geography Today Bk 3 – there was a prep on watersheds that evening – when Alice Hodges from Remove skated over the glassy boards into Vb form room. 'Antonia *Pen*rose – you're wanted in the st*u*dy'. She sang this with relish and then skated away again.

The study, which was also Miss Church's drawing-room, was furnished with highly-polished Edwardian Sheraton pieces and Persian rugs. There was an ornate break-fronted bookcase full of unappetising books on one side of the fireplace, and the wall opposite to where she now stood, her back to the double doors, was taken up by a mullioned bay window, from which she could see the top of the latticed stone terrace wall and beyond it yellowing lawns sloping down to the tennis courts, on the left, and The Military Building, a leftover from the Army's occupation of the house during the war, on the right. In this dark and draughty shed (its north side was entirely open to the elements) which had a tarmacadam floor that minced your knees if you fell over, they played team games with bean bags when the weather was considered too bad for tennis or lacrosse.

Miss Church faced her from a chintz-covered armchair by the fire. She had a smallish, square head, a beaky nose and highly-coloured cheeks. Her hair, cut like a man's at the back, was thick and wiry and not yet entirely grey, and it stuck out in tufts above her ears. The head sat oddly on a huge unfit body that tended to wobble in an unpleasant way when she walked and was always draped in loose navy or maroon garments, uninfluenced by fashion of any period and peculiar to Miss Church.

She had once seen a photograph of Miss Church as a young woman during the first world war. It was difficult to think of the thin and flat-chested person who held a boat-shaped tennis racquet with what looked like purpose, and who smiled at the camera from under an amusing hat, as having anything to do with the headmistress she knew. Miss Church taught English literature and scripture. She had a habit, when seated before the class, of holding her fountain pen vertically and letting her thumb and index finger

56

slip down it to the nib. She would then about-turn the pen very slowly, tapping on the table as she did so. The action was usually accompanied by some ominously quiet instructions, apparently directed to the book in front of her: 'Jessica. I believe you learned the Gospel according to St Mark, Chapter 4, for preparation. Would you,' a pause, 'and she would look up at this point with a little smile that was not a smile at all, 'recite verses 10–23 for me please, darling.'

Miss Church did her pen trick now, tapping it on the notebook in her lap. She did this for some moments and then put the pen down on a little table which, when visiting parents were present, sometimes supported minute glasses of dry sherry. She opened the notebook. There was a small yellow envelope between its pages which she handed to Antonia. 'What does this mean, darling?' Miss Church asked her.

She unfolded the telegram – it had already been opened – and read: 'All is performed stop arent I a good sister Fran'.

'Yippee,' she said, and did a little jump. Miss Church looked at her unsmilingly. 'Children are not permitted to receive telegrams here,' she said, 'except on matters of the utmost gravity. I should like some explanation, please.'

She did not fancy telling Miss Church about Noel and his Song Book and what she'd asked Fran to do. It was not Miss Church's business. 'It's a private matter. Nothing to do with school,' she said brightly. 'I see,' said Miss Church, turning a nasty shade of purple. 'I'm afraid you are a rather silly and superficial person, Antonia. I think you like to imagine yourself as different from other people, superior in some way. I have to say I have not found your work to be superior. You tend to run away from anything at all difficult.' There was a pause, during which she felt uncomfortable for a moment, knowing that Miss Church referred to the music exam she'd been supposed to take last term but had refused, at the last minute, to sit because she knew she'd fail.

'It is perhaps your parents' fault that you are spineless and spoonfed,' Miss Church went on, 'but if you can't cure this you will never achieve anything very much.'

Out of the window she could see a group of figures straggling up from the tennis courts. Caroline Timpson, or it might have been Rosemary Bailey – it was hard to tell from this distance – was bouncing a tennis ball on her racquet. Every so often the ball bounced out of the racquet's reach and rolled away over the tussocky lawn, and Caroline – or Rosemary – chased after it. Meanwhile, Miss Church was winding up: 'You will be late for your preparation, Antonia, and must do an extra half hour. Before you return to your classroom, run up to Matron, will you, and tell her I'm sorry to have to bother her – I know how busy she is – but that I had to send you for a clean tunic because your own is so,' she looked briefly at the lentil soup and ink stains on the brown serge bosom, and then turned away, 'soiled'.

She had to wait until December 25th for the Song Book, which Fran said was her Christmas present. She made Fran go endlessly through her experience in the Times Bookshop. There had been a long queue. Noel had sat at a large table, piled with books, signing away. He'd worn a grey pinstripe suit, a pink shirt, a navy blue and white spotted bow-tie. When her turn had come, she'd said: 'Would you sign my book please?' and he'd said: 'It will be a pleasure.' When he'd signed his name, which he did rather fast in blue biro, she said 'Thank you very much' and he'd said: 'Not at all.'

The book when it came was large and important-looking, the paper cover designed, not very well she thought, by G.E. Calthrop. The signature was eccentric and ran diagonally across the title page, fitting neatly between 'The Noel Coward Song Book' in large lettering at the top, and 'London, Michael Joseph' in much smaller print at the bottom. The flourish of the 'd' in Coward sliced through 'with an introduction and annotations by Noel Coward'. On the facing page was a portrait by Clemence Dane of Noel in a yellow jumper. His hair was unflatteringly short. His forehead and ears looked pink and cross, and his pursed mouth was a bright lipstick red.

She ran her fingers over the signature as though it had been in braille. His ballpoint pen had nearly pierced the paper on some strokes; how nearly was obvious when she turned the page over. He had written this with his pen. She copied the signature again and again in her rough notebook and was soon able to execute a perfect forgery and at speed.

It dawned on her gradually that Noel was never going to be interested in the real Antonia Penrose, who at fourteen was not just fat but spotty and greasy-haired and uncomfortably like Mrs. Worthington's daughter. He could only be drawn to the Antonia Penrose she had invented for him, who was thin, attractive (not beautiful: she hadn't thought that necessary) and talented in the same sort of ways that he was. The only chance she had of winning, if not his love, then at least his respect, was by *doing* something. She removed a new exercise book from the form room cupboard and started work on a play. It was to be a musical play, she decided. She called it *Court Circular* and it centred on the social round and marital difficulties, two subjects she knew next to nothing about, of a couple in their thirties whose names were Paul and Theresa Felton.

Getting the dialogue to sound convincing wasn't as easy as she'd anticipated. But she enjoyed writing the songs, or lyrics as she always thought of them (as in 'book and lyrics by so-and-so'), and she composed the tunes and fitted the words to them while walking round and round the lacrosse pitch while supposedly 'off games'. 'Off games' was the expression employed by the school to denote the first three days of the your 'period'. 'Period' was the word Matron used for what your mother called 'the curse'.

Of the songs *Queen of Sheba:*

I think you're the Queen of Sheba,
You know I do
And somehow I sort of feel a
Passion for you.
I don't care if the Atlantic's between us

So long as it's still romantic between us
I think you're a bit of my heaven come true –

had perhaps the best tune, but the smartest lyric was undoubtedly
When the Moon is Blue:

When the moon is blue, darling,
I'll be true, darling, to you.
There are quite a few, honey,
Apart from you, honey,
I'm fond of too.
But I'll be faithful sometime,
You may be sure
When I've had my fun time,
Then I'll be your
Baby
When the moon is blue, darling
I'll be true, darling,
To you

The cover of her notebook said: *Court Circular,* A Musical Play
in Three Acts, but she ran out of steam after the first Act and wrote
nothing more. Noel was not to know this, however. She copied
the First Act into a new notebook and wrote him a letter:

Dear Mr Coward,
I thought you might be interested to see the first Act of my new
musical play, *Court Circular* . . .

He would be obliged to reply now, if only to return her
manuscript, and for weeks she believed this, sometimes racing to
the Junior Room – the mail was given out there – at break,
sometimes staying edgily in her form room in the hope that the
prefect in charge of the mail would seek her out: 'Huge envelope
for you, Antonia'. 'Oh thanks,' would be her bored reply as she
took the packet without even glancing at it. It was years before she
realized that he probably received hundreds of unsolicited
manuscripts a week, and that the only ones that had even a hope of

being returned, possibly accompanied by a discouraging note from a member of his staff, were those which had self-addressed and stamped envelopes attached to them.

The silence that greeted *Court Circular* marked the end of her obsession as it had been. She still loved him, and she still wrote to him sometimes, but she never posted the letters. What she did post to him, every year, was a birthday card, drawn and painted by herself. The wording never varied: 'To the Master, With best wishes for a Happy Birthday, from Antonia Penrose.' She always wrote her address on the bottom left hand corner, just in case, but she no longer expected a reply. What was permitted was to picture him at breakfast, slitting the heaped envelopes with a silver paperknife. He hurried through them until he came to hers, exclaimed with pleasure, called everyone round to look, and then stood the card up in a place of honour on the piano.

One December when she was nineteen and teaching English and Art at a girls' preparatory school – a post she had no qualification for and had managed to get because her parents knew one of the governors – she read in the paper that he was ill in bed at the Dorchester Hotel. She read this on the 13th. There were three days to go before the birthday. She took great pains with the card, an ink and wash drawing, rather Cecil Beatonish, of an Edwardian couple walking in a park. The woman held a parasol and a little dog on a lead. Behind the couple, who walked arm in arm, was a suggestion of railings and a park bench. She pasted the picture onto a stiff blue card and wrote inside: 'To the Master. Happy Birthday. I hope you're feeling better'. She was about to sign her name as usual when she hesitated, and wrote *Anthony* Penrose instead.

Two days later she was just setting off for the school when the post arrived. Among a pile of stuff for her parents, there were two other items: a communication for her from Lloyds Bank which she did not open, and a white, square envelope addressed in blue type to Anthony Penrose, esq., The Glebe House, Monkerswell, nr Salisbury. She opened it quickly and took out a greetings card. Its entire front was taken up by a black and white photograph of

61

Noel. He was sitting cross-legged in a white tubular chair on top of a rock in the middle of the sea. He wore a dark jacket and white trousers and espadrilles and he had a book on his knee. It was impossible to tell what book. He was seated sideways to the camera, his face half towards it with an amused expression that was not quite a smile. She opened the card. At the top, a blue seal, the sort some people stick on Christmas parcels, said: 'Merry Xmas' in fancy silver lettering above two silver holly leaves and berries. Underneath this was a signature: Noel, in red biro. There was nothing else at all.

This card, and how she came by it, became in time her 'Noel Coward story', and she told it through the years at what she judged to be the right time to the right company. It was not a story that improved with embellishment. It depended for its effect – gratifying hilarious, nine times out of ten – on a fast Coward delivery:

> Cue (approximate): 'As Noel Coward might say . . . '
> A: I can't remember if I ever told you my Noel Coward Story?
> Cue: No. Do tell.
> A: I was madly in love with him from about the age of eight and used to write to him from school, and ring him up – SLOane 2965 – and always for his birthday I drew him a card and he never replied. And then one year when I was about nineteen I did him a rather Cecil Beatonish card – he was in bed at the Dorchester with 'flu – and I wrote 'To the Master' at the top as usual, and was just about to sign my name 'Antonia Penrose' when I stopped and wrote Anthony Penrose instead. And I got a reply by return of post.

She felt no disloyalty at telling this story, being certain that, if he could hear it, he'd laugh louder and longer than anyone else.

She had been married to James for six years and had had three of her five children when the Great Coward Revival began in the mid-nineteen sixties. She went twice to see him – his last stage appearance – in *Suite In Three Keys*. Separated from him by only the orchestra pit she was shocked to discover how like her own father, who had died the year before, he was, not just in obvious physical ways of height and shape (their ears were almost identical) but in facial expression, in speech – particularly delivery and timing – and in gesture. The way Noel sat in an armchair, for instance, one leg crossed over at the knee, his arms stretched along the chair arms, fingers lightly drumming the ends, was at once familiar, as was the way he held a cigarette, the way he inhaled smoke and released it, the way he nodded his head in emphasis. None of these similarities had been discernible from photographs. He seemed, curiously, to be more like her father – whom she had loved but had never bothered to get to know until it was too late – than her father had been himself.

Sometimes she and the children had Noel Nostalgia Evenings, when she played them all her old scratched 78s. Flora, in particular, was attentive and appreciative. 'I really love Noel,' she said once, but Flora loved lots of things, and most people. James always absented himself from Noel Nostalgia Evenings, either going to bed earlier than usual, or shutting himself in the study with his dictaphone and his in-tray.

She thought about Noel whenever his name was mentioned in the press or on the wireless which was increasingly often. They were not real thoughts, more a feeling of tenderness. It was comforting to know that he was alive somewhere, getting up in the morning, cleaning his teeth, eating, making jokes. Nothing too terrible could happen to a world that contained him. But he was old and, according to reports, often ill. The day could not be far off that she dreaded when she'd turn on the wireless unsuspectingly and hear a newsreader announce: Sir Noel Coward died today at his home in Jamaica (or Switzerland; or wherever he happened to be), and then, after a brief biography, go on to give the cricket scores, as though the world were still the same place.

She was glad that he was being fêted in his old age, though a part of her felt resentful that he was everybody's darling now. There was nothing special or peculiar or different about loving Noel

63

Coward. Even his critics had stopped being critical and seemed to think that everything he'd ever written was bloody marvellous. This was surely insulting, and a mistake she'd never made, even at ten years old.

When Christina, whom she had not seen for years, telephoned and suggested they go together to see *Cowardy Custard* at the Mermaid, she was tempted to refuse. Only Noel Coward could sing a Noel Coward song. She did not want to see a camp chorus perform dance routines with top hats and canes or hear them wreck his songs by sticking too closely to the melody in places where he would sing seconds or merely speak the lines. But she went because it would be nice to get away from James and the children for once, and she enjoyed herself because it was fun seeing Christina (fat now, hooray, whereas she had remained eight stone five – except during her pregnancies – for the past twenty years). *Cowardy Custard* itself was exactly as she'd thought it would be.

Three weeks later she got back from the afternoon school run to find a note stuck in one of the children's gumboots outside the front door:

> Your telephone's out of order. We've got one spare ticket for *Cowardy Custard* on the 17th, and knowing your passion for N.C. thought of you. Please come if James can spare you. Supper in the Garrick afterwards.

After a little thought – it was very kind of the Evanses to ask her and she didn't want to seem ungrateful –she refused the invitation, explaining that James had already spared her once to see it, and suggesting the ticket should go to someone who hadn't because it was a wonderful . . . (she paused here, because the word 'show' was so disagreeable, but how else could she describe it?). She also said, which was true, that there was a parent-teacher meeting at Flora's school that evening, and that she ought to be there. Flora's maths being what they were.

On the morning of the eighteenth she had washed up the breakfast things, wiped some surfaces, made the beds (Jack's had to be stripped because he'd wet his sheets without telling), collected socks and knickers from the floor of every bedroom and put them in the dirty linen basket, stared out of Flora's bedroom window unseeingly for half an hour, wished she were dead, and was just about to start on the mountain of ironing she'd been avoiding for days because it was all tangled up with laddered tights and matted and odd socks, when the telephone rang. She recognized Jane Evans's voice:

'Antonia – It's Jane here. I can hardly bear to tell you this, but we were sitting in our seats at the Mermaid yesterday just before the curtain went up, when NOEL COWARD walked into our row and sat down in the seat next to yours – I mean the one you'd have been in. He got a standing ovation. The whole theatre clapped and roared for at least ten minutes. He was on his own and seemed very frail and old and his hands shook and he wept throughout the entire performance. It was rather upsetting, really, but wonderful too, of course. You never did meet him, did you? And if you'd been there you'd have sat NEXT TO HIM,' (she shouted this). 'I really can't bear it!'

After Jane had rung off, she sat on her bed and stared at the floor. Tears, for sad Noel and for herself, spilled over and ran, slowly at first and then faster and faster, down her cheeks. They fell onto a join in the carpet that had come unstuck, its edges curled back to reveal the underlay. The carpet, once a subtle shade of blue, was grubby now, and needed not just hoovering but a good going over on hands and knees with a sponge and a bucket of *1001*, something she'd been putting off for months.

People for Lunch

'I must get up,' Mrs Nightingale said, but did not move. During the night she had worked her way down the bed so that her feet were now resting on the brass rail at its end. Two years ago today it had been Edward's feet striking this same brass rail with peculiar force that had woken her. 'I don't feel well,' he'd said, and she'd replied – sleepily? sharply? – she needed to know but could not remember – 'Then you'd better not go to work today.' When he'd gone on, haltingly, to murmur: 'No. I can't,' she'd sat up, wide awake and afraid. For Edward was a workaholic. Nothing prevented him going to the office. She'd leant over him and seen that his face and neck were beaded with sweat. She'd touched his forehead and found it as cold and green as marble. 'I've got a pain,' he said, 'in my chest.' Each word was a single, concentrated effort. 'I can't breathe.' Stumbling to the telephone which lived on Edward's side of the bed, she'd started to panic. How could she explain to the doctor, probably still in bed and asleep, how serious it was with Edward lying beside her listening? It was then that she'd begun to shake, and her teeth to rattle in her jaw like pebbles in a bag. She'd knocked the telephone directory on to the floor and misdialled the number half a dozen times. (It was not true that anxious, panicky people proved themselves level-headed under fire.) 'Be calm, Fanny. Go at it slowly,' Edward had said, lying still, his eyes unfocussed on the ceiling.

A shuddering sigh on Mrs Nightingale's left made her turn her head. Lying close on the adjoining pillow was the face of Bone.

The dog's small body was concealed by the duvet, as was Mrs Nightingale's own. Mrs Nightingale stared at Bone's black nose, at the white whiskers that sprouted from her muzzle and chin, at her short sandy eyelashes. Bone's eyes were shut, but the left ear was open, its flap splayed on the pillow to reveal an intricacy of shiny and waxy pink coils. Mrs Nightingale leant across and blew gently in this ear. Bone opened one eye and shut it again. Mrs Nightingale put her arms round Bone and laid her head against the dog's neck. It smelt faintly of chicken soup. Bone jerked her head away and stretched her legs so that her claws lodged themselves in Mrs Nightingale's stomach. Mrs Nightingale kissed Bone on the muzzle just above the black, shiny lip. Bone opened her jaws wide in a foetid yawn and stretched again and went back to sleep. Mrs Nightingale got out of bed and left Bone, still covered to her neck by the duvet, sleeping peacefully.

Bone was not allowed in beds, only on them, and she reminded the dog of this. 'I don't like dogs,' she added untruthfully. The house was very quiet. Mrs Nightingale walked out bare-footed on to the uncarpeted landing and stood for a moment listening to the inharmonious ticking of the clocks downstairs. There was no sound from her children's bedrooms and their doors were uninvitingly shut. 'I hate being a widow,' she said aloud.

The bathroom door was blocked by a wrinkled dustbin sack full to overflowing with clothes intended for a jumble sale. She dragged it out of the way. From its torn side hung the yellowing arm of a Viyella cricket shirt. From its top protruded a brown Harris tweed skirt. Liza's name was still stitched to the tiny waistband. Had she ever really been that size? Mrs Nightingale had meant, before the move, to unpick the nametape from Liza's old uniform and take it back to the school for resale, but there had never been the time. This black sack was one of many about the house. Before moving she'd labelled them as to contents, but on examination recently they all contained the same things: out-grown clothes, single football boots, curtains originally made for Georgian sash windows that would not fit the small casements here, curtain hooks, picture hooks, bent wire coat hangers.

Lying motionless in the bath Mrs Nightingale saw Edward on the stretcher being carried into the ambulance. He had joked with the ambulance men. She would never forgive him for that. It had been his joking, and the doctor saying on arrival, just before he'd sent her out of the room: 'If you move, Edward, you're a dead man. If you lie still and do exactly what I say, you'll be all right,' that had given her hope. She could see Edward now, calling out from the stretcher to the twins, shivering in their night things on the front door step: 'Be good, monkeys. I'll be back soon.' And she could see herself, wrapped in his dressing gown, bending down to kiss his cold cheek before the ambulance doors closed. She'd wanted to go with him, she'd needed to go with him, but had had to wait for her mother to come and look after the twins.

The bath water was by now tepid and Mrs Nightingale's finger ends were white and shrunk. As she lay there, unable to move, the church bells began a faint tolling through the shut window and at once the image of the ambulance with its frenetic blue light turning out of the drive was replaced by a picture of dead tulips and lilac in the vase beneath the lectern. She'd seen these on Friday when she'd gone to the church to check the Flower Rota List and found her name down for this Sunday. She forced herself out of the bath and pounded down the passage to Liza's room. She shook the mound of bedclothes.

'Liza – did you remember to do the church flowers yesterday?'

Liza was gliding through a dark lake on the back of a sea-serpent. She opened blank blue eyes for a second and then shut them again.

'Did you do the church flowers?'

The eyes opened again, flickered and then closed. Waking was a trial for Liza.

'Liza – '

'No. I didn't. Sorry.'

'You're the absolute end.' Mrs Nightingale was furious. 'You asked what you could do to help and I said – '

71

'Sorry, Mum.'

'You're not asked to do much. And you're eighteen, not six.'

'Don't flap,' – Liza's voice sounded as though it had been dredged from the bottom of a deep lake – 'the congregation's geriatric. No-one will notice if the flowers are dead.' She yawned. 'You're sopping wet,' she said incuriously to her mother.

'I need your help,' Mrs Nightingale cried. 'Get up at once, now, before you fall asleep again.' She stood for a moment awaiting results, but as there were none, left the room banging the door behind her.

Mrs Nightingale visited the twins' room next. They were fast asleep on their backs. Lily, on the camp bed they took turns for, was snoring.

'Wake up, both of you,' Mrs Nightingale said. She trampled over their discarded clothes. 'Wake up now.' They sat up slowly, looking hurt and puzzled. 'It's late,' Mrs Nightingale said, 'Nine o'clock. They'll be here by half past twelve and there's a lot to do. You must get up. Now.'

'Who'll be here?' Poppy asked.

'Nine o'clock isn't late, it's early,' Lily said. 'It's Sunday.'

'Now,' Mrs Nightingale said and left the room.

When Mrs Nightingale opened Dave's door he was propped on one elbow, reading. His hair, which had been recently cut by a fellow student using blunt nail scissors, stuck out in stiff tufts. Here and there patches of scalp were visible. They'd had a row about the hair when he arrived. Usually Mrs Nightingale cut Dave's hair, and when she did he looked very nice. This present cut, which he'd admitted he wasn't that keen on himself, was an example of the perversity her son was given to and that Mrs Nightingale found exasperating and incomprehensible. He glanced up at her as she came in.

'Hallo, Mamma. How are you, darlin'?'

The question took Mrs Nightingale off-guard. Suddenly, she wanted to tell him. She wanted to say: 'Daddy died two years ago today.' She wanted to collapse on Dave's bed and howl, perhaps all day, perhaps for ever. Instead she stayed in the middle of the room and stared at the row of hats that hung from hooks above Dave's bed and which, together with the accents – foreign, regional – he adopted, formed part of her son's disguise kit.

'If you're awake, why aren't you up?' Mrs Nightingale heard herself say.

'Stay cool,' Dave said. 'I'm just tucking into Elizabeth Bishop.' He waved a paperback in the air that his mother recognised as her own and removed from its shelf without permission.

'How do you rate her? Compared to Lowell . . . ?'

'Get up, please,' Mrs Nightingale said.

'Okay, Marlene. Tuck in.'

Marlene, the second syllable of which was pronounced to rhyme with Jean, was not Mrs Nightingale's name, which was Frances. Marlene, which sometimes became Marlena, second syllable to rhyme with Gina, was the name Dave had bestowed on his mother some years ago when she'd started regularly cutting his hair. 'I'm due for a visit to Marlene's salon,' he'd say, ringing her from Leeds. 'Is the head stylist available?'

Mrs Nightingale moved backwards to Dave's door and fell over the bicycle wheel she'd noted on her way in and taken care to avoid.

'Shit. And your room's in shit, Dave.'

'Cool it.'

'Look, it is in shit and it smells. Do you have to sleep with the window shut? Why are you wearing that tee-shirt in bed?'

'I haven't any pyjamas, that's why,' Dave said reasonably.

'I know if I leave now you'll just go on reading – ' Mrs Nightingale was getting desperate – 'so get out now, while I'm here.'

'I will as soon as you go. I've got nothing on below this tee-shirt, and the sight of my amazing, user-friendly equipment might unsettle you for the day. Tuck in, Marlene.' He yawned, showing a white tongue and all his fillings, and stretched his huge arms above his head.

Mrs Nightingale returned to her bedroom and dressed herself in scruffy, everyday clothes. Then she pulled Bone out of the bed and swept the bottom sheet with her hands. Being white, Bone's hairs did not show up well against the sheet but Mrs Nightingale knew they were there, and sure enough they flew around the room and settled on the floorboards like snowflakes in a paperweight snowstorm. Mrs Nightingale straightened the duvet and banged the pillows while Bone sat on her haunches, sorrowfully watching. As soon as the lace cover was on Bone leapt back on the bed and made herself comfortable among the cushions. Mrs Nightingale looked at her watch. This time two years ago she had just arrived at the hospital having driven at ninety most of the way. There'd been nowhere to park so she'd parked in one of the doctors' spaces. 'You can't park there,' an old man planting out geraniums by the hospital steps had told her, having watched her manoeuvre. Three floors up, on Harnham Ward, Sister had looked up from her notes and said: 'The specialist has examined your husband and would like to see you now.' Mrs Nightingale suddenly remembered the specialist's nose, aquiline and messily freckled. She'd stared at it as they sat opposite each other, divided by a desk. 'He's on the edge of a precipice,' the specialist had said. 'It was an almost total infarct – that means the supply of blood and oxygen to the heart has been severely reduced. A large part of the heart muscle is already dead. The next forty-eight hours will be crucial. If he survives, and I can give you no assurances, the dead muscle will be replaced in time by scar tissue, which is very tough and can do the same sort of job – '

I hate doctors, Mrs Nightingale thought as she went downstairs. Hate them. She took one look at the kitchen, then shut the door and went into the drawing-room, a room too poky to deserve the title that, from the habit of a lifetime, she had given it. It smelled of soot and damp and cigarettes, and of something indefinable that might have been the previous owners. Mrs Nightingale got down on her knees in front of the fireplace and swept the wood ash and cigarette stubs she found there into a dome. She stuck a firelighter on top of this, but the log baskets, were empty except for two pieces of bark and several families of woodlice, so she got up again and started to punch the sofa cushions into shape. Dave came in while she was doing this. He was still wearing the tee-shirt but to his lower half he'd now added an Indian tablecloth which he'd wrapped twice round himself and tucked in at the waist.

'You left a filthy mess in the kitchen last night,' Mrs Nightingale said, remembering the slag heap of coffee grounds decorated by a rusty Brillo pad on the kitchen table. 'I thought you were going to get dressed.'

'Liza's in the bathroom.' Dave scratched his armpit, then sat down heavily on the sofa cushions and rested his head on his knees.

'Dave, I've just done that sofa. We've got people for lunch – '

'Yup. Sure thing. Sorry. What can I do?' He stayed where he was and Mrs Nightingale stared, mesmerized, at his large yellow feet. The toenails were black and torn. Black wire sprouted from his big toes. The same wire twined his calves, visible beneath the tablecloth. It stopped at the ankles, but continued, Mrs Nightingale knew, beyond his knees to his thighs, where it no longer twined, but curled. It was impossible that this huge male person had ever been inside her body. 'Well, the log baskets are empty, as you see,' Mrs Nightingale said, 'so when you're dressed – '

'Sure, sure.'

'I did ask you, you know,' Mrs Nightingale bravely continued, 'when you arrived, if you'd be responsible for getting the wood in, and you said – '

'Yeah. Yeah. Sure. Yup. Tuck in.' He sat for a moment longer and then got up, hitching the tablecloth which had slipped a little. He looked round the room. 'I like your little house, Marlene.'

'It isn't *my* house.' Mrs Nightingale was hurt by Dave's choice of possessive adjective. 'It's *our* house. It's home.'

'Yup.'

'No chance, I suppose,' she said as he padded to the door, 'of your wearing your contact lenses at lunch?' Dave stopped dead in his tracks and turned sharply. 'What's wrong with my specs?' He whipped them off and examined them myopically, close to his nose. They were bright scarlet with butterfly sides, the sort typists wore in the Fifties. One arm was attached to the frame by a grubby selotape bandage.

'Nothing's wrong with them. It's just that you look nicer without them. You're quite nice looking, so it seems a shame – '

'Oh Christ,' Dave said and then hit his head on the beam above the door. 'Fuck. I hit my head everywhere I go in this fucking house. Cottage. Hen coop. Hovel.'

By the time Mrs Nightingale had finished scrubbing the potatoes they were all down in the kitchen with her. The kitchen was too small for five people comfortably to be in at one time. She had once, when they were all tripping over each other, made this observation and had received a long lecture from Dave on the living conditions of the average farm-labourer and his family in the latter part of the nineteenth century. Her son was nothing if not inconsistent, Mrs Nightingale thought, remembering the hen coop remark.

'Who's finished the Shreddies?' Poppy was on her knees on the brick floor, peering in a cupboard.

'Dave had them last night – don't you remember?' Liza said, sawing at a grapefruit with the bread knife. A pool of cloudy juice and pips spread over the table, soaking an unpaid telephone bill. Mrs Nightingale snatched it up.

'Here, have this' – Liza plonked the grapefruit halves into bowls and handed one of them to Poppy. 'This is better for you. You're too fat for cereal.'

'Speak for yourself, you great spotty oaf. At least I haven't got suppurating zits all over my face – '

'You will soon,' Dave interrupted cheerfully. 'You're into a pubescent exploding-hormone situation. Tuck in.'

'If you had, they might detract from your nose which, by the way,' – Liza glanced at it casually – 'is one big blackhead.'

There was a skirmish. Mrs Nightingale caught the milk bottle as it leapt from the table.

'Cool it, girls.' Dave had seen his mother's face. 'Marlene's trying to get organized. Aren't you Marlene?' He was propped against the Rayburn, dressed now in one of his father's city shirts and scarlet trousers, the bottoms of which were tucked into old school games stockings, one brilliantly striped, the other grey, and shovelling Weetabix into his mouth from a bowl held within an inch of his face. Each time the spoon went in it banged horribly against his teeth. 'Is the Rayburn *meant* to be off?' he asked, mock-innocently, between mouthfuls.

Mrs Nightingale was about to burst into tears.

'What? Out of my way please.' She pushed the red legs to one side, and knelt on the dog bed in front of the stove. Inside an erratic flame flickered. She turned the thermostat as high as it would go.

'Why's the heat gone down?'

'How the fuck should I know? The wind, probably – '

'Don't swear, Mummy,' Poppy said, grabbing a banana from the fruit bowl and stripping it.

'Put that banana back! It's for lunch.'

'We've got rhubarb crumble for lunch. I made it yesterday, remember.' Poppy took a bite out of the banana, folded the skin over the end and replaced it in the fruit bowl on top of a shrivelled orange.

'Look,' Mrs Nightingale said, 'we'll never be ready at this rate. Couldn't you all just – '

'Keep calm, Mamma. Sit down a moment and drink this.' Liza handed her mother a mug of coffee. 'There's nothing to do. Really. They won't be here till one at the earliest. All we've got to do is get the joint in – '

'Are we eating animals? Yuk. Unreal. Animals are people – '

'Shut up, Lily. – Do the spuds and the veg and lay the table and light the fire and pick some flowers – five minutes at the most.'

'The whole house is in chaos,' Mrs Nightingale said, 'it's composed of nothing but tea chests and plastic bags.'

'They're not coming to see the house. They know we've only just moved. They're coming to see *you*.'

'Actually, they're coming to inspect our reduced circumstances,' Dave said in a prissy voice. He picked up a piece of toast and stretched for the marmalade. Mrs Nightingale pushed it out of his reach. 'No, you've had enough.'

'Daddy couldn't bear them,' Lily said, staring into space.

'Couldn't bear who?' Poppy paused at the door.

'The Hendersons, stupid.'

'The Hendersons? Are *they* coming to lunch? Unreal.'

'Where do you think you're going to, Poppy? You haven't cleared up your breakfast things – '

'I'm going to the lav, if you must know. I'm coming back.'

'While you're up there, Fatso, take some of the gunge off your face!' Dave shouted at her.

'Have you got the logs in?' Mrs Nightingale asked Dave, knowing that he hadn't.

'I'm just about to. We shouldn't *need* a fire in May,' he said, resentfully as though his mother were to blame for the weather. 'Right, Marlena.' He rubbed his hands. 'Here we go -o,' he added in the manner of an air hostess about to deposit a snack on the knees of a passenger. He sat down on Poppy's chair and pulled a pair of canvas boots from under the table. A lace snapped as he put them on.

'Are you going to shave before they arrive?' Mrs Nightingale asked, eyeing him.

'Dunno. Oi moigh.' – Dave rubbed his chin so that it rasped – 'an' yere agine oi moigh 'na'. Don't you like me looking manly and virile?' Mrs Nightingale said No, she didn't much. No.

'Mrs Henderson will, though. She's got a yen for me. She'll really tuck in.'

'Oh ha ha,' Liza snorted from the sink.

'Mr Henderson has too. He's always putting his arm round my shoulder. Squeezing me. Kissing – '

'I don't suppose he's that desperate to get herpes. He hasn't seen you since you were about ten – '

'Do something for me, Lil, would you,' Mrs Nightingale said, as Dave minced from the room flexing his biceps. Lily sighed. Did she know what today was? Mrs Nightingale thought perhaps she did. It was impossible to get near Lily at the moment. She resented everything her mother said and did, prefacing her argument with 'Daddy always said' or 'Daddy would have agreed with me that . . . ' She'd been in a sulk since the move because the cottage was thatched i.e. spooky, witchy, bug-infested – and because her father had never been in it. 'Wake up, there,' – Mrs Nightingale waved her hand slowly up and down in front of Lily's face. Lily managed not to blink.

'Go and get Bone off my bed and put her out. She hasn't had a pee yet.' Lily went on sitting there, expressionless. Then all of a sudden she leapt up, scraping back her chair, and ran out of the room.

'Bone, Bone, my darling one, I'm coming.' They could hear her clattering up the stairs, calling 'Bone, beloved angel, Bone – '

'She's mad,' Liza said, stacking plates in the rack. 'All my family's mad. And Dave is completely off the wall.' Mrs Nightingale kissed Liza's spotty face, pink and damp with steam. 'I love you, Lize.' she said.

As Mrs Nightingale rooted in the kitchen drawer looking for enough knives to lay the dining-room table with, Dave's face appeared at the window above the sink. He flattened his nose against the pane and drummed on it with his fingers. 'Open up! Open up!' he shouted. Liza leaned across the taps and biffed the window. It opened in a rush. Dave's face disappeared for a second, and then reappeared half in the window. 'Ladies,' he said with a South London inflexion and in confidential tones, holding up what looked like a piece of string and dangling it from between his fingers and thumb, 'do your hubbies' jock-straps pass the window test? If not – ' he leered and let go of the jock-strap which fell across the sill and draped itself over the hot tap, and then held up a packet of something: 'Try new Weedol! Fast-acting, rainproof and guaranteed to eradicate all biological stains for an entire season. Just one sac*chette*' – he paused to consult the packet – 'treats 160 yards, or – if you ladies prefer a more up-to-date terminology – 135 square metres, of normally soiled jock-straps.' He backed away from the window, creased with laughter, and tripped over a flower pot.

'Pathetic,' Liza said, tugging at the window catch, 'quite pathetic.'

'Logs!' Mrs Nightingale shouted at him, just before the window jerked to, scattering them with raindrops, 'Logs, logs, logs!'

Mrs Nightingale did her best with the dining-room which, not being a room they had so far needed to use, had become a dumping ground. There were ten full tea chests stacked in one corner, her husband's golf clubs in a khaki bag, a clothes horse, innumerable lampshades and a depressed-looking cockatoo under a glass dome. Beneath the window precariously stacked books awaited the bookshelves Dave had promised to put up in the summer holidays. Everything in the room, including a dining-table much too large for it, was deep in dust. Mrs Nightingale looked at her watch. This time two years ago she'd sat beside Edward, who'd lain on his back without pillows, his chest and arms wired to a machine. Attached to the machine was a cardiograph that measured and recorded his heartbeat. The signal had gone all over the place, sometimes shooting to the top of the screen, and the bleeps, at each beat, had been similarly erratic – six, say, in succession followed by a silence which, each time it occurred, she'd felt would never be broken. 'The heroin was delicious,' Ed had murmured in a moment of consciousness, 'it took all the pain away, but they won't let me have any more in case I get hooked.' Why couldn't you have died at once, Mrs Nightingale thought, remembering her agony watching the nurse adjusting the drip, which had kept getting stuck, and checking the leads on Ed's chest which, because he rolled around a lot, were in constant danger of coming loose. This had happened once, when there'd been no nurse in the room. She'd been on the edge of her chair, her eyes alternately on Ed, and on the screen, when suddenly the bleeps had stopped and the signal had flattened into a straight, horizontal line. A red light had come on at the side of the machine and with it a whine like the unobtainable tone when you dial. He's dead, she'd thought. Sister had rushed in at once and checked Ed's pulse and then the leads and after a minute or two the crazy signal was back and the bleeps. 'Try not to worry, dear,' Sister had said. 'Worrying doesn't help.'

Mrs Nightingale forced herself out of her chair and went in search of a duster.

'The joint's in the oven,' Liza said. She had an apron on which bore the message I Hate Cooking, and was standing at the stove stirring a saucepan. 'I'm making onion sauce.' She looked up. 'Are you okay, Ma?' By way of an answer Mrs Nightingale enquired if anyone had seen the silver anywhere. Poppy knew. She and Lily were scraping carrots and glaring at each other across the kitchen table. She got up and helped her mother drag the despatch box from under the sink in the washroom. Back in the dining-room she stood and watched her mother dust the table.

'Mum – can I have a friend to stay – Julia, I mean, in the holidays?'

'Maybe. If we're straighter by then.' Mrs Nightingale didn't like Julia. On the child's last visit Mrs Nightingale had caught her in her clothes cupboard, examining the labels and checking to see how many pairs of Gucci shoes Mrs Nightingale owned, which was none. Mrs Nightingale didn't own a Gucci watch, either, and evidently wasn't worth speaking to: Julia hadn't addressed one word to her in five days. She'd managed a few indirect hits, though, as when at breakfast one morning, having accepted without comment the plate of scrambled eggs Mrs Nightingale had handed her, she'd leaned on one elbow to enquire of Poppy: 'Presumably your mother will be racing at Goodwood next week?' Mrs Nightingale was damned if she'd have Julia to stay again.

'I get bored without a friend,' Poppy moaned on. Mrs Nightingale wasn't having any of that. 'You can't be bored,' she said, 'and you've got Lily.' She unwrapped a yellowing candlestick from a piece of yellowing newspaper. 'Here, take this.'

'We don't get on,' Poppy said. 'We've got nothing in common.' That was rubbish, Mrs Nightingale told her.

'It isn't rubbish. She's so moody. She never speaks – just sits and stares.'

Since the truth of this could not be denied, Mrs Nightingale changed tack:

'As a matter of fact you don't deserve to have a friend to stay.' Poppy put down the spoon she'd been tentatively rubbing with a duster and stared at her mother with her mouth open.

'Your half-term report is the worst yet,' Mrs Nightingale continued, 'and we ought to discuss it. Not now. I don't mean now. Later. This evening, perhaps, when they've gone.'

'Miss Ansell doesn't like me. It's not my fault.'

'It isn't just Miss Ansell,' Mrs Nightingale said, more in sorrow than in anger. 'No one, no one – apart from Miss Whatsername – you know, games mistress – had a good word to say about you. You won't get a single 'O' Level at this rate. Lily, on the other hand – '

'*Don't* compare me with her. She's quite different to me.'

'Different *from* me. Yes. She knows how to work, for one thing. And she reads. You never open a book.'

'I do.'

'The Beano annual. And you're *thirteen*.'

Poppy grinned sheepishly at that. 'Oh, Muzkin,' she said, and sidled up to her mother and put her arms round her waist.

'Muzkin nothing,' Mrs Nightingale said, disentangling herself. For it really was worrying. Poppy never did open a book. If ever she happened by some mischance to pick one up, she'd drop it again as soon as she'd realized her mistake. As a result of this her ignorance went wide and deep. Mrs Nightingale spent sleepless nights discussing the problem with Bone.

Liza's head appeared round the dining-room door.

'Bone's eaten the Brie, I'm afraid,' Liza said, 'so there's only mousetrap for lunch.'

'Where is she? I'll kill her!' Mrs Nightingale cried preparing to do so.

'I've already beaten her,' Liza said. 'It's my business, she's my dog.'

Not when it comes to spending millions of pounds a year on Chum and Butch and Winalot and vet's bills, Mrs Nightingale thought. Not when it comes to clearing up mountains of dog sick and dog shit. Then she's my dog. She followed Liza back to the kitchen. 'Where's Dave?' she asked crossly. 'Where's the wood?'

'He's gone to get some milk and the papers,' Liza said, knowing what her mother's reaction would be.

'*What?*'

'I asked him to go because we're out of milk and you'll want the papers so that the Hendersons can read them after lunch.'

'Has he taken my car?' Mrs Nightingale was beside herself.

'Of course he's taken your car. How else would he go?'

Mrs Nightingale hated Dave taking her car. She hated him taking it because being stuck up a track with rusty bicycles the only means of escape made her feel a prisoner. She hated him taking it because he hadn't asked permission and because she didn't trust him not to drive like a racing driver – i.e. a maniac. It was her car. She hated Dave too because he ought to have remembered what the day was. There was something wrong with him that he hadn't. Something very wrong indeed.

'He has no business to take my car,' she said, 'he'll be gone for hours.'

Liza was taking glasses out of a cupboard. 'Don't be stupid,' she said briskly. 'He'll be back in a minute. He's only gone for the papers, for God's sake. He was *trying* to be helpful.' She held a glass up to the light. 'These glasses are filthy. I'd better wash them.'

'Get up, Lily,' Mrs Nightingale was now in a state of rage and panic. Lily was lying in the dog bed on top of Bone, kissing Bone's ears. 'Get up! Have you made your bed and tidied your room?'

'You can't make a camp bed.' Lily got up reluctantly, her navy jersey angora now covered with dog hairs.

'Answer that, would you, on your way,' Mrs Nightingale snapped as the telephone rang from the drawing-room. Lily returned almost at once.

'It's Granny.She wants to talk to *you*.'

'Fuck,' Mrs Nightingale said. 'Didn't you tell her we've got people for lunch?' Lily shrugged. 'Well,go back and tell her I'm frantic – '

'I'll say,' murmured Liza, putting glasses on a tray. 'These glasses are gross – did you get them from the garage?'

' – and that I'll ring her after tea. Go *on*. Hurry.'

'Granny sounded a bit hurt,' Lily said when she came back, 'She said to tell you she was thinking about you today.'

'What for?' Liza said.

What for, Mrs Nightingale repeated to herself, what for – ? 'What can Dave be doing?' she said, 'He's been gone for hours.' She opened the oven door. The joint seemed to be sizzling satisfactorily.

'Stop flapping,' Liza said.

'Did you put garlic on the joint? And rosemary? I couldn't see any.'

'Of course. Stop flapping.'

'Poppy, you're *soaked*! Couldn't you have worn a mac?' Poppy squelched into the kitchen and dumped a collection of sodden wild flowers on the table.

'*I* was going to do the flowers,' Liza said.

'God, the gratitude you get in this place,' Poppy fingered the limp cluster. 'What are these?'

'Ladies' smocks. *Must* you do that in here?' Liza said as Poppy found an assortment of jugs and lined them up on the table. 'I'm trying to get lunch. You can't put wallflowers in with that lot,' she added in disgust.

'Why can't I?' Poppy wanted to know.

84

'Because they're orange, stupid.'

'Piss off. I like them. I like the *smell*.'

Mrs Nightingale left her daughters to it and took the tray of glasses into the dining-room. Perhaps Dave *had* had an accident. Perhaps, at this very moment, firemen were fighting to cut his lifeless body from the wreckage. That was all she needed. It was typical of him to put her in this position of anxiety today of all days. 'If he's alive I'll kill him,' she thought aloud, knowing that when – please God – he did walk in she'd feel nothing but relief. As she went back into the kitchen he came in by the other door, accompanied by a smell of deep frying. The Sunday papers and two cartons of long-life milk were crushed against his chest. He uncrossed his arms and unloaded their contents into the watery mess of broken stems and leaves on the kitchen table.

'Hey – mind my flowers,' Poppy said. She sniffed. 'I can smell chips.'

'Whoops. Sorry.' Dave straightened up and caught sight of his mother. 'Hi there, Marlene.' He licked his fingers, slowly and deliberately. 'Finger fuckin' good,' he said when he'd finished. There was a silence, succeeded by a snort of laughter from Liza, succeeded by another silence.

'Dave, could I have a word with you, please – ' Mrs Nightingale spoke through clenched teeth. She jerked her thumb towards the door. 'Outside.'

'Righto, Marlena.' He snatched up the *Observer* and followed his mother into the hall.

'Watch out, Dave,' Poppy sang out after him. 'You're in deep trouble, Boyo.'

'What are you so screwed-up about?' Dave asked when Mrs Nightingale, determined that they shouldn't be overheard, had shut the drawing-room door. Dave plonked himself into the nearest arm chair.

'Get up out of that chair! Put that newspaper down!' Dave got up, very slowly. 'Take that smirk off your face!' Mrs Nightingale shouted. He towered above her, shifting from one foot to the other, while his eyes examined the ceiling with interest. 'I've had you,' Mrs Nightingale went on, her voice shaking. 'I wish you weren't here. You're twenty years old. You're the only so-called man in this house. I should be able to look to you for help and support. You had no business to take my car without asking – '

'Liza said we were out of milk – '

'It's not her car. It's *mine*. And *I*'d asked you to get the wood in. That's *all* I asked you to do. All all *all*!'

'Oh come *on* – '

'I won't come on.' Mrs Nightingale's voice rose. 'You were gone for hours while everyone else was working. Did you really eat chips, by the way?'

'I was hungry, I'm a big boy,' Dave said, perhaps hoping to appeal to that need (he supposed all women had) to mother and protect huge grown men as though they were babies.

'You didn't have breakfast till ten. And it'll be lunchtime any minute. You can't have been hungry.' Dave said nothing. He was bored with this interview and showed it by jiggling his knee 'That finger business wasn't funny,' Mrs Nightingale said. 'It was disgusting. How could you, in front of Lily and Poppy?'

'Lily wasn't in the kitchen, actually,' Dave said. He started to pace about with his head down, a sure sign that he was losing his temper.

'Don't be pedantic with me, Dave.' Dave stopped pacing and swung round and pointed his finger at his mother in a threatening fashion.

'Fuck *you*,' he said. 'You're a complete hypocrite. No one in this house uses filthier language than you. It's ''shit this'' and ''bugger that'' all fucking day. We took the words in with your milk – ' There was a pause, during which Mrs Nightingale considered reminding him that the twins, at least, had been bottle-fed, but Dave was quite capable of turning this fact to his advantage, so she said nothing. 'Well, I'm sick of your dramas and panics,' he continued, warming to his theme of self-justification. 'I can't stand the atmosphere in this place. I can't *work* here. I'm going back to Leeds. My tutor didn't want me to take time off to help you, and I've missed two important lectures already.' He made for the door.

'Typical,' Mrs Nightingale said, taking care not to say 'fucking well typical' as she would normally have done. 'You can't take any sort of criticism, ever. You just shout abuse and then walk out – it's too easy. What's more, you haven't been any help to me at all. You haven't lifted a finger – '

'Mum,' – Liza's head appeared round the door as Dave reached it. He took two steps backwards – 'Shouldn't you be putting your face on? It's after twelve.'

'Go away,' Mrs Nightingale said, 'I'm talking to Dave.'

'Sounds like it. Poor Dave.' Liza's head withdrew. The door banged shut.

Mrs Nightingale and her son stood in silence, both waiting for something. Dave stared at the floor and at the front page of the *Observer* which lay at his feet. He pushed at it with the toe of one green canvas boot.

'Sorry I was rude,' he said at last without looking up.

Mrs. Nightingale gave a sigh. Dave was good at apologies – much better than she was – and sometimes indulged in them for days after a particularly bloody row, castigating himself and telling anyone who'd listen what a shit he'd been. The trouble was, the apologies changed nothing, as Mrs Nightingale had learned. They never prevented his being rude and aggressive (and unfair, she thought, *unfair*) next time round. She didn't want his apologies. She wanted him to stop the behaviour that made them necessary. She watched him now get down on his knees and take off his specs and rub them on a dirty red-and-white spotted handkerchief and put them back on his nose. He picked up the *Observer* with his left hand and then struck at it with the fist of his right.

'I'm going to kill Mrs Thatcher,' he said, 'listen to this – ' Oh dear, thought Mrs Nightingale.

Dave and newspapers did not mix. Cruise missiles, violence in inner cities, child abuse, drug abuse, vivisection, famine, rape, murder, abortion, multiple births, divorce rate, pollution, terrorism, persecution of Blacks and homosexuals, sex discrimination, unemployment, pornography, police brutality, rate capping – the stuff that newspapers were made of – were a daily cross he bore alone. 'You can't take the whole burden of the world on your shoulders,' she'd tell him when he rang from a Leeds call box desperate over the destruction of South American rain forests, or the plight of the latest hi-jack victims. 'The world has always been a terrible place,' she'd say, 'we just know more about it now because of the media. Horror used to be more *local*.' Then – since it seemed important to end on a positive note – she'd go on to remind him of ways in which the world had changed for the better, instancing the huge advances made in medicine this century (T.B. and polio virtually wiped out, infant mortality and death in childbirth negligible, etc) and reminding him that there were salmon in the Thames these days, and that people could fall into the river and swallow whole bucketfuls of its waters and not die. 'Try and get a sense of proportion,' she'd say, something she'd never managed herself. She knew that when she lectured Dave it was herself she was trying to comfort. The world was a far nastier place than it'd been when she was a child, even though there'd been a world war going on for some of that time. Far nastier.

Thinking about all this she was spared hearing Mrs Thatcher's latest pronouncement, although it was impossible to miss the passion in Dave's recital of the same. She came to when he stopped in mid-sentence, and put the paper down.

'It's the twenty-third today,' he said, 'Did you realize?'

'I know,' Mrs Nightingale said.

'Oh, Mum, I'm sorry. Why didn't you say?'

Dave, on his knees, began to rock backwards and forwards, his arms folded across his stomach. 'Poor old Dad, poor old Dad,' he said. Then he burst into tears. Mrs Nightingale got down on her knees beside her son. She put her arm round his shoulders which reeked of wet wool and chipped potatoes. She sensed that he did not want her arms round him but did not know how to extricate himself. After several minutes he blew his nose on the red-spotted handkerchief and licked at the tears which were running down his chin.

'I must get the wood in and light the fire.' He disengaged himself and got up. 'Then I'll shave. Sorry, Mum.' He gave her a pale smile. At the door he turned, and said in a sharper tone: 'But I still don't understand why you didn't *say*. And why didn't we go to church this morning – or did you, before we were up?'

'No,' Mrs Nightingale said.

'And why are the fucking Hendersons coming to lunch? You don't like them and Pa couldn't stand them. None of it makes sense.' He shook his head, spraying the room with water like a wet dog.

'Look, Dave,' Mrs Nightingale began. She explained that she hadn't asked the Hendersons, they'd asked themselves. She couldn't put them off for ever. Also she'd thought that having people to lunch might make the day easier in some way. And as for church – well, he didn't like Rite A any more than she did. It always put them into a rage, so there was no point, was there, in going.

'True,' Dave said.

It *was* true, she told him. But what she thought they might do, once they'd got rid of the Hendersons, was drive up to the churchyard and take Poppy's flowers perhaps, and put them on Daddy's grave.

Dave's eyes started to fill again. ' . . . and then go to Evensong in the Cathedral, if there's time. It'll be a proper service with proper singing and anthems and sung responses.'

'Yup. Cool.'

'All right, sweetheart?' Dave nodded and fiddled with his watchstrap, a thin piece of canvas, once red and white striped. 'I suppose you realize,' Mrs Nightingale lied, 'that when I asked you to give me a hand this week, it was just an excuse for wanting you here today. I needed you.' But perhaps it was not a lie, she thought. Perhaps, subconsciously, she had needed him.

'I'm getting the wood now,' Dave said. He peered out of a dismal mullioned window, against which a yew branch flapped in the gale. 'I think the rain's stopping.'

The kitchen when Mrs Nightingale entered it was clean and tidy, everything washed up and put away. Liza was taking off her apron.

'All done,' she said.

She was a wonder, Mrs Nightingale told her, a real star.

'Mum you must get changed, they'll be here – '

Mrs Nightingale stopped in the doorway. 'Lize – do you know what today is?'

'It's the day Daddy died,' Liza said. 'Go on, Mum, I'll come and talk to you when I've done the ice.'

The back door banged as Mrs Nightingale climbed the stairs. She could hear Dave's grunts as he humped the log baskets into the hall. It was a relief to be on her own for five minutes. She needed to be alone with Edward who – she stood on the dark landing and peered at her watch – this time two years ago had been about to leave her. Suddenly, without warning and without saying goodbye. Not even a look. Not even a pressure of the hand. She'd hated him for this, until it had dawned on her that it was inevitable. He'd been hopeless at partings. The number of times she'd driven him to Heathrow and been rewarded not with hugs and the 'I'll miss you, darlings' and 'take care of your precious selves' other people seemed to get, but with a preoccupied peck and then his backview disappearing through the barrier. 'Turn round and wave, you bugger,' she used to will him, but he never did.

'You two ready?' she called, in hopeless competition with Madness, through the twin's bedroom door. Then she opened her own. The room looked as though burglars had visited it. The drawers of both clothes chests had been wrenched out; garments spilled from them onto the floor. A brassière, its strap looped

90

round a wooden drawer knob, trailed greyly to the rug where two leather belts lay like coiled springs. Mrs Nightingale turned her gaze to the dressing table. Here unnumbered treasures drooped from every drawer and orifice. The surface of the table was littered with screws of cotton wool and with unstoppered scent bottles, from which all London, Paris and New York disagreeably breathed. A cylinder of moisturizing lotion lay on its side oozing cucumber extract into the contents of her jewel case which sat, open and empty, on the stool. Three cotton wool buds, their ends clotted with ear wax, had been placed in the china tray which normally housed Mrs Nightingale's lipsticks. Only two lipsticks remained in the tray; the rest, which had been torn apart and abandoned with their tongues protruding, were jumbled up with beads and cotton wool. Mrs Nightingale recognized her daughter Poppy's hand in all this. She opened her mouth wide in anger and despair, but no sound came. Instead, the telephone screamed from the table by her bed. When after the eighth ring no one had answered downstairs, Mrs Nightingale picked up the receiver.

'Mrs Nightingale? Mr Selby-Willis here.'

'Oh hallo, Jerry,' Mrs Nightingale said. (Fuck fuck fuck fuck fuck). 'How are you?'

'How are *you*?' Jerry Selby-Willis asked, in his best bedroom drawl.

'Well if you must know, I'm frantic. I've got people arriving for lunch any minute.'

'One normally does on a Sunday. Grania's just gone off to the station to meet our lot. I can't imagine *you* being frantic about anything – '

'It just goes to show how little – '

'When are you going to have luncheon with me?' Jerry Selby-Willis interrupted her. 'Or dinner?'

'Jerry, I've only *just* moved house – ' Mrs Nightingale began. She had accepted none of his invitations. ' Then you're in need of a nice, relaxing dinner. Tuesday. Have you got your diary there?'

'No. Look, I'm afraid I must go. I haven't got my face on – '

'I'll ring you tomorrow, from the office.'

She must remember to leave the telephone off the hook tomorrow, Mrs Nightingale thought, as she wrenched garments from hangers, tried them on, examined the result in the looking glass, and tore them off again. Or else get the children to answer the telephone and say she was out.

'I've got nothing to wear!' she wailed, as Liza came into the room.

'That looks fine,' Liza said. 'Where's your hairbrush?'

While Liza brushed her mother's hair, Mrs Nightingale perched on the dressing-table stool and searched for her blue beads.

'I can't find my blue beads,' she said, turning out another drawer.

'Poppy's wearing them,' Liza said. 'She said you said she could. Time you dyed your hair, I think, or else made with the *Grecian 2000*,' she said kindly, putting the brush down.

'I think I heard a car,' Mrs Nightingale said, 'do you think you could round everyone up and go down and tell the Hendersons I'm coming. Give them a drink.'

Alone, Mrs Nightingale looked at her watch. It was ten past one. Edward was dead. He'd been dead a full quarter of an hour. At five to one, no doubt when she'd been fending off Jerry Selby-Willis, the signal on the cardiograph had flattened into a straight line for real this time, and the bleeps had ceased. She had not kept vigil; she had not been with him, holding his hand. She sat on the stool, twisting her wedding ring round and round her finger, for comfort. When at last she lifted her head she caught her reflection in the glass and was dismayed to see how pinched and wary and closed her face had become. 'Things have got to get better,' she said aloud. 'I must make them better.' There was a little moisturizer left in the bottle. She squeezed some into her palm and rubbed it into her forehead and cheeks, into the slack skin under her chin, into her crêpey neck. 'I am alive,' she said, 'I am not old. I am a young woman. I could live for another forty years yet.' She

92

fumbled for the blusher, and worked it into her cheeks. 'I am a *person*,' she said threateningly into the glass. 'I am me, Frances.'

There was a thundering on the stairs, followed by Dave, out of breath at the door.

'Hi, folks, it's Lamborghini time,' he hissed. 'The Hendersons are in an arriving situation.' He had not shaved, after all, but on the other hand he was not wearing his red secretary spectacles either. You could not have everything, Mrs Nightingale supposed.

'Hurry up, Marlene,' he said. 'You can't leave us alone with them.' He vanished, and then immediately reappeared. 'You should know that Mrs H. is wearing a salmon two-piece, with turquoise accessories. Tuck in.'

Mrs Nightingale grabbed a lipstick from the table and stretched her mouth into the grimace that, with her, always preceded its application. At the first pressure the lipstick, which had been broken by Poppy earlier and stuck back by her into its case, toppled and fell, grazing Mrs Nightingale's chin as it did so with a long gash of *Wicked Rose*.

Deathcap

After I'd killed my wife I went downstairs and made myself a cup of tea. My hands shook as I spooned the tea leaves into the pot, and later, when I poured out, a few drops splashed the table-cloth, clean on that morning. But the giddiness had gone, and apart from the slight shaking I've mentioned, I have to say I felt calm – empty as the grey sky outside the window, but calm. 'It's going to be all right,' I told myself as I sat at the kitchen table, dredging the cup with a spoon (my wife had neglected to return the tea strainer to its drawer).

'It's going to be all right,' I repeated, louder this time but with perhaps a shade less conviction – for the future escaped my efforts to confront it, drifting away like the steam from my cup. As I sat there, it was the past, in random images, that began to fill up the emptiness. Here was my wife Angie on our wedding day, assisting me to cut the cake, attired in an old-fashioned navy two-piece that had belonged to her mother. Its buttons were new, purchased by my wife and sewn on by her the day before our nuptials.

'Old, borrowed, blue *and* new,' she'd said to her sister, 'that can't be bad.'

'I hope you're right, Ange, I definitely hope you're right – we all do,' Helen had said, meaning they all knew she was making a mistake.

What they were hoping for was to be able to say *I told you so* in a couple of months' time. For it could hardly work, could it – marriage between a thirty-six-year-old school teacher and a trainee bank clerk, a mere boy of nineteen?

I sat on at the table, holding my cup in both hands, my elbows resting on the table-cloth. I saw us on honeymoon, huddled in a rented cottage near Swansea. It had been so cold we'd had to take the curtains down and pile them on the bed, and no inside toilet meant that by the end of the week we'd been a rash of nettle stings acquired on nocturnal visits to the water closet at the end of the garden. I saw myself leaning over my wife's shoulder, watching her mark the exercise books she brought home every evening to the flat above the electricians we lived in the first three years of our marriage, before I got promotion. She was a tough marker, and I saw her now in the lamplight, scoring through whole paragraphs, underlining mistakes with a red biro, putting SP in the margin, or a question mark. One time, she'd written at the bottom of the page: 'This is nonsense. Come and see me about it after school.' 'Please Miss,' I'd murmured into her hair. 'Please Miss, may I come and see you after school?'

I drained my cup and got up to pour another. Through the open door I could see my wife's luggage, one small suitcase, packed and ready in the hall. On the hall shelf was her ticket to Lyme Regis. Only the day before, my wife, who eight weeks earlier had undergone a hysterectomy from which she'd been slow to recover, had caught the milkman on the front doorstep.

'I'm going away tomorrow,' she told him, 'to the seaside for a fortnight, and my husband will only require one pint every other day.'

From the hallway I'd seen the milkman replace his crate on the step and note the change of order on his pad. 'Looks like we're in for an Indian summer,' he said, slipping his pencil behind his ear. 'Should be nice at the sea.' He lifted his head and sniffed, as though he could detect salt on the breeze. 'Mornin',' he greeted me as I emerged into the sunshine and strode past him on my way to the car. At the gate I swung my briefcase in salute.

'Will you be back for tea?' my wife called out in a faint, post-operative voice.

'Thought she meant me for a moment, guv,' the milkman said,

and then we all laughed – the milkman heading towards me down the path, myself unlocking the car door, and my wife, thin and pale in her dressing-gown, on the front doorstep.

We'd bought her train ticket late that afternoon, on my return from the bank. First I'd driven her to the chemist in the High Street for some necessaries, then we'd walked the short distance to the bookshop, with a view to obtaining some paperback holiday reading. She'd hung on to my arm, and I'd had to slow up a bit. 'Silly, isn't it,' my wife confided, 'but I still feel as though I were made of cotton wool.'

In the shop she didn't seem to know what she wanted, just 'something to get me out of myself, nothing heavy.' The assistant hadn't been any use. He stayed behind the counter and gestured vaguely at the shelves. In the end my wife chose a couple of historical novels, by women authors, and a who-dunnit. 'That'll do,' she said, 'I read so slowly these days.'

'Half a mo,' I said, suddenly inspired, 'What about *The French Lieutenant's Woman?* Just the ticket as you're off to Lyme Regis.'

'I wasn't that keen on the film,' my wife said.

'Have you a copy of *The French Lieutenant's Woman?*' I asked the assistant who was busy reading. He came to at that, and put down *Exchange & Mart* and got off his stool and came round our side of the counter.

'I'm sure we have, sir,' he said, all authority now, ignoring my frown. 'The Le Carrés are over here.'

I ask you! He didn't even have the grace to blush when I pointed out his mistake, nor again when I found the book for him – merely shrugged.

'You win some, you lose some,' he said cheerfully as he rang up the till.

'You'll lose all your customers, matey, that's for sure!' I told him, snatching the parcel and propelling my wife out of the door.

My wife was silent in the car going home. 'We'll go back via the station,' I told her, turning left instead of right out of Fish Street, 'It'll save time and bother if we get your ticket now.'

All this had happened yesterday, less than twenty-four hours ago. Thinking about it, looking for clues and portents, I realized I hadn't drunk my second cup of tea. It had gone cold and scummy and there was a fly struggling on its surface. As I tipped it down the sink, the giddiness returned, and I had to grip the taps for support. It lasted only a moment or two, a swimming, spinning sensation like the vertigo that accompanies a fear of heights, and when it subsided I was left with an urgent need to relieve myself.

Attending to the calls of nature necessitates a trip upstairs to the bathroom, passing the bedroom en route. I hastily undid my laces, removed my shoes, and then crept up the staircase in my socks, levering myself on the bannister rail as I did so. The bedroom door was just ajar. The curtains were drawn across, but even in the dim light I could see the dishevelled bed with the eiderdown half off, trailing to the floor, and a straggle of hair escaping from the pillow. Without making a sound I pulled the door to and then tiptoed along the passage to the bathroom.

Mission accomplished, I was standing before the bathroom window, chasing a sliver of soap round the wash-basin, when a movement in the garden below caught my eye. I parted the curtains and peered down. Unlatching the wicket gate in the hedge that separated our back premises, stepping through it, pausing to examine the state of our runner beans, and now, walking purposefully down our path, armed with a basket, was Pam Mason, our neighbour and a close friend of my wife's. I gave my hands a perfunctory wipe, and then crept back along the passage and down the stairs. I had reached the back door and opened it before Pam had a chance to knock.

'Saw you coming,' I said, but the words did not sound as breezy as I'd intended, and my voice sounded unfamiliar and shrill, like a woman's voice.

'I promised to give Angie these,' Pam said. She held up the basket in which I could see a sheaf of knitting patterns and some balls of peach-coloured wool. I put out my hand to take the basket, but she held on to it.

100

'Mind if I come in? I'd like to have a word and wish her all the best – is she all packed up?'

I hesitated for a moment, disconcerted by Pam's questions and by her gaze which had fixed itself on my feet.

'She's in the land of Nod at present,' I said, putting a finger to my lips, 'but do enter, by all means. Would you care for a cup of something?'

'Asleep?' Pam looked at her watch. 'At this hour?' She followed me through the utility room to the kitchen, and placed her basket on the formica worktop.

'Have a pew,' I said, moving nimbly to the kettle in my stockinged feet. The phone rang from the hall.

'Better answer that,' Pam said, 'or it'll wake Angie.'

It was my wife's sister on the phone, something I hadn't bargained for. 'She's just popped out, Helen,' I told her, 'for some last minute shopping – shall I get her to buzz you back?'

'Don't trouble her,' my wife's sister said, 'just remind me again the time of her train.'

'3.32,' I said, 'arriving Lyme Regis 6.29.'

Back in the kitchen, I put my shoes on, placing each foot in turn on a chair seat while I tightened the laces.

'I took the liberty of making the coffee while you were on the phone,' Pam said, watching me, 'but I didn't sugar yours.'

'Cheers,' I said. I dropped two sugar lumps in the cup, and then sat down opposite her, at the table.

'What's up with Angie?' Pam said, plucking a piece of fluff from the beige cardigan she always seemed to be wearing whenever I saw her. 'I thought you said she was still in bed?'

'Correct,' I said, 'but Helen would've taken on if I'd told her that. Angie didn't sleep last night,' I explained, 'and I knew she'd never manage the journey without any shuteye, so I advised her to stay put. She took a sleeping tablet at six.'

'You've had a worrying time, Ken, haven't you?' Pam's tone was quite pleasant for once (for I knew she'd never liked me. It showed in hundreds of ways, but mostly it was her tone of voice –

brisk, offhand – whenever she addressed a remark in my direction. And she never would look at my face, always to the left or right of it. I used to mind. I used to say to Angie in the early days: 'Your friend Pam doesn't go a bundle on me,' – but I'd long since given up caring). I shrugged, to indicate Yes, I had had a worrying time, but I could handle it. Pam leaned towards me across the table.

'No, I mean it Ken, you need a holiday after all you've been through. It's a shame you can't go with her.'

I said nothing. Until the operation, my wife and I had never spent a night apart in thirteen years of marriage. I'd wanted to go with her to Lyme, even though it meant a fortnight of Helen, but I'd taken my holiday, all of it and more, when she'd come out of hospital, so that I could look after her.

' . . . she's on the mend now, I'm sure,' Pam was saying, after something I hadn't caught, 'even if she isn't picking up *quite* as fast as Doctor said she would.'

Silly bitch, I thought, you silly, silly bitch. 'She's lost over two stone,' I said flatly, and I remembered the way my wife used to be, well-covered, not to say plump – and energetic, always on the go. Suddenly I saw the bed upstairs, with that untidy hair, my wife's hair, on the pillow. I put my head down quickly and took a swig of coffee.

'You okay, Ken?' Pam said when I looked up. 'Perhaps I shouldn't tell tales out of school, but Angie's really concerned about you, you know. She says you haven't been yourself this last couple of weeks. She's afraid the strain's telling on you, that you may be heading for some sort of, well, how shall I put it, breakdown, or something.'

I've killed my wife, I told Pam silently, I've killed Angie.

'Nothing wrong with me,' I said, 'I'm right as rain.'

Pam pushed herself up from the table. 'Well, I'd best be off now,' she said, 'seeing as Ange is not available. We're going over to Mother's today, even Bob. Makes a change.'

Pam was a golf widow at weekends, I knew, but I wasn't going to say anything supportive. If she and Bob didn't enjoy the close relationship Angie and I had always shared, it was hardly my fault. Or my business. I got up to see her to the door, but in the utility room she stopped and turned round and looked at me, actually looked at me, and her face was bright red.

'I feel I should tell you, Kenneth,' she said, 'that Bob and I reckon you've been a good husband to Ange over this operation. I don't mind admitting I never thought you'd stick with her, and I told Angie as much. Have an affair with him by all means, if you must, I told her, but don't marry him. Okay, so he needs a mother at the moment, and you fit the bill, but soon as he grows up and knows what he's missing, he'll be off, you'll see – '

'I'd never leave her,' I said, swallowing hard, as though the action itself might in some way aid the digestion of Pam's unpalatable home truths. 'She knows I'd never leave her.'

'That's what I'm trying to tell you,' Pam said. 'I was wrong. And all those flowers you bought her – ' she laid her hand on my arm, and her pebble eyes were misty ' – this place looked like a florist's shop when she came out of hospital.'

A florist's shop, I thought, and immediately I saw the girls in Murphy's off the High Street, snipping and tying and stripping stems of their leaves. Only this time the girls' deft fingers were weaving the flowers, white lilies and freesias, into wreaths, and pressing them into crosses shaped from damp moss.

'Cheerio, then,' Pam was saying. 'If there's anything you need while Angie's away, give us a shout. Oh, I'd better have that basket back – ' After I'd fetched it, I stood and watched her until she was halfway down the path.

I came inside, and washed up the tea and coffee cups and tidied the kitchen. I swept the floor and emptied the rubbish bin into a plastic sack and put the sack outside the back door. Then I went through to the living-room. I vacuumed the carpet and emptied the ashtrays and dusted the ornaments and photographs. I blew on the plastic dahlias and crysanths the kids in Angie's class at the Middle School had sent round after the operation. They'd stuck the flowers into a birch log, polished in carpentry by one of the boys, which bore the message *An Autumn Bouquet* in burnt-on lettering round the base. All this time I kept a weather eye on Bob's Sierra, parked in the road. Eventually they came out, and Bob mustered his troops down the path – Pam in front with their two youngest, Jimmy and John, and bringing up the rear Stephen, their skinny fifteen-year-old, shouldering a fishing rod. I was glad my wife couldn't witness this family outing, too good to be true, like a scene from a telly commercial. She'd wanted children, they were part of her decision to marry me, I couldn't kid myself they weren't – and all I'd given her were four miscarriages. 'I'm too old, Kenny,' she'd said after the last one, six years ago, 'I'm just too old. You should've married someone younger.' But I hadn't wanted children – except to please her – and I'd never wanted someone younger, only Angie.

I stood back from the window and watched as Bob swivelled round to check the passenger doors. He wound the window down, pulled on his seat belt, and the car drew away from the kerb and out of view. Even though I'd been waiting for them to go, it wasn't a good feeling when they'd gone, knowing there was no one next door, no human creature beyond the wall that separated their lives from ours. As I stacked the cleaning things in the cupboard under the stairs, I pictured their silent rooms: unmade beds in the poky boxrooms the boys made do with; abandoned toys on the living-room floor; congealing breakfast dishes piled in the sink. In the hall I stood still for a moment, one hand on the bannisters, looking up the dark stair-well listening. There was no sound. I collected my car keys from the ledge, stepped round my wife's small tartan suitcase, and went out through the front door.

I left the Saturday car washers and shoppers and drove away from the centre of town to the wooded residential hills on its outskirts. When I reached the Forestry Commission land bordering the golf course, I backed the car on to the verge, exchanged my shoes for boots, and then began walking up a muddy track overhung with yellowing silver birches. I'd never walked there before without

Angie, and it seemed strange, and lonely, just as I'd known it would be. I tried to concentrate on the problem, the problem of how and where I was going to dispose of her.

The question had come up before, more than once, on this very walk. We'd be strolling along arm in arm, chatting about this and that, when suddenly I'd stop and say: 'If I did away with you, here, now, no one would ever find out.'

'Yes they would,' my wife would argue. 'We passed that man with the Great Danes earlier – he'd remember seeing us. Like as not you'd meet him again on the way back, and he'd wonder where I'd got to. Then, when he'd seen the headlines – '

'I could do it on a day we hadn't met anyone,' I'd insist, parting the rhododendrons to point at the jungle beyond, where gorse, heather, bracken, holly bushes, infant oaks and Christmas trees all struggled to free themselves from the stranglehold of ivy and bramble. 'I'd encourage you to explore that undergrowth – on the pretext of searching for rare orchids or edible fungi – then I'd kill you and bury you there.'

'Tracker dogs,' Angie'd say, unimpressed, 'there are such things as tracker dogs. You'd never get away with it. Anyway, husbands are always the first suspects when wives go missing. Even good husbands.'

On one occasion we'd come across a Deathcap, half-hidden in the bracken. 'Look at that,' I said, decapitating it with my toe. 'Look at those evil white gills. I could slice this and fry it for your breakfast, mixed in with mushrooms. It would seem like an accident.'

'Not if you didn't die too, it wouldn't,' Angie said. 'Anyhow, as you know, I don't eat a cooked breakfast.'

'Supper then,' I went on, relentless. I had a morbid imagination, my wife told me. I should have been a crime writer or an actor, not a bank official.

'Perhaps all this nonsense is a cover-up,' she said, squinting at me through her thick hair. 'Perhaps you really do want to get rid of me.'

'That's it, my dear,' I murmured – and Vincent Price couldn't have played it more sinister – 'it's a double bluff.' I placed my fingers round her neck and squeezed.

'Don't,' my wife said, pulling away from me, 'don't.' She hated her neck being touched.

In the car going home she asked me why I did it, why I kept on doing it. It was just a game, I told her, I'd played it with my brother when we were small, it was only a game.

'No, seriously, Kenny, I want to know. I used to think it was funny, but you do it too often.'

'Okay,' I said, inventing fast to pacify her. 'You know what it's like at the top of a ladder, or on the edge of a cliff, when you're frightened of falling? What you want to do most, so that you can't fall, is jump. Right? Well, under this macho exterior is a little lad who's constantly afraid he'll lose you, that you'll go off with somone else or die – so a part of him wants to kill you first, to prevent it happening. Q.E.D.' I laughed. I was pretty pleased with this solution, trotted out like that, unpremeditated – nonsense of course, yet plausible enough in all truth. But my wife didn't seem to be, and she didn't laugh, as I thought she would.

'I don't know, Ken,' she said as we drew up in front of the house, 'but what I do know is I'm fed up with that game, so could we give it a miss for a bit? It's beginning to give me the creeps.'

Thinking about all this, I found I'd walked further than I'd intended to, and I turned round and started back. I'd met no one, unusual for a Saturday. As I walked, I examined the woodland, hoping for a suitable burial ground to present itself. Burying my wife wasn't going to be easy, it occurred to me. I wouldn't be able to carry, or drag her far, and driving the Cavalier any distance up the track was impossible because of the mud. And supposing I didn't get stuck, there was the problem of tyre marks, no doubt easily identifiable. Husbands were always the first suspects, my wife had said, even good husbands. Would the neighbours, would anyone, testify to my being a good husband? The milkman, maybe, and okay, so Pam seemed to have come round to me at last, but there was a backlog of thirteen years' mistrust she'd be bound to revert to. 'Never liked him,' I heard her say between sobs, 'never trusted him, the bastard.' Then there were all those loose ends I'd given no proper thought to: How was I to get my wife's body out of the house and into the car without being seen? How could I be certain to get her out of the car and into the wood? I saw the courtroom at the local assizes, and myself in the dock staring straight ahead, my knuckles whitening on the rail.

You say you put her on a train, the 3.32 for Lyme Regis?
Yes.
Yet no one remembers seeing either of you at the station, and the ticket collector recalls no one answering your wife's description on the train.
I put her on the train.
How do you account for the fact that the tickets you say you purchased for your wife on the evening of Friday, the twenty third, was never handed in at Lyme Regis?
All I know is, I put her on the train.
And that she never arrived at her sister's house, where she was expected?
I don't know.
Perhaps you would care to explain to the jury why you told your neighbours that your wife had telephoned from her sister's on the evening of the twenty-fourth, to say that she'd arrived safely and was settled in . . . ?

I began to sweat then. It was dark in the wood, the sky overcast, ready to rain, and I walked faster, keeping my head down in order to avoid the brackish puddles in the ruts. I didn't see them until I was almost upon them – two tweedy crones with walking sticks, and an overweight sealyham nosing in the bracken. I kept going, not slackening my pace at all, and they moved to the bank as I approached and leant on their sticks, waiting for me to pass. I knew they were staring at me. As I drew level, one of them said something I couldn't catch.

107

I sat in the car for a long time, leaning my head on the steering wheel, with my eyes closed. I tried to focus my mind on Angie, on our past and my future, but I couldn't fix on anything. When the rain started, in a cloudburst, pummelling the roof and bonnet, cascading down the windscreen with the force of an automat car wash, I switched on the engine and the wipers, and drove home.

At the front gate I stopped, and stood still in the rain, and stared up at the house and saw it as a stranger might. It looked solid and normal, an ordinary semi like its neighbours – half orange brick, half stained pebbledash; green windows, green down pipes and guttering; a clematis (*Jackmanii*, I'd given Angie for her fortieth) strung over the porch. Yet as I stared, the house faded to a black and white photograph, to smudged newsprint with an arrow and a caption. I clicked the gate shut and walked up the path.

'Some Indian summer,' my wife said. She was dressed in the blue paisley frock I'd bought her to go on holiday, and had her back to me, bent over the stove. The ridges of her spine showed clearly through the thin wool. 'Where'd you get yourself to, Ken?' she said. 'Do you realize what the time is? You did say you'd wake me at one, remember.'

'Angie,' I heard a voice say. It was my voice, or a tape recording of my voice. 'Angie – '

She turned round then. 'What is it, Kenny? What's happened?'

I knew, a part of myself knew, that something had to be said, that explanations were required. But I'd gone too far with it this time. I couldn't get back. Even when she came over to me, it wasn't me who stood there, hands stiffly at his sides, but a dummy, just someone who looked like me.

From a long way off I watched her take the dummy's hands in hers and chafe them. She put her arms round his waist and held him.

'You can tell me, Kenny,' she said, 'you can tell me. You can tell Ange.' And very gently she laid her head against his chest and kept it there, as though listening for a heart beat.

Tales from the Spare Room

Whenever they are invited to, they play cards with the maids in the maids' sitting-room.

Alice has got the Queen, Barbara says, pointing a finger at Alice who retreats into the sofa clutching her cards close to her face, so that Barbara shan't see them.

Barbara leans across and tweaks a card from Alice's hand. She looks at it and pouts and pulls her bottom lip and then raises her eyes to the ceiling in what seems to be despair; and then she slots the card into her own hand and spreads the cards into a fan. Mollie and Lucy, on the other side of the table, and on chairs, snigger. Hee hee, Barbara's got it now, Lucy says. Hee hee hee.

Fooled yer, Barbara says. She whips two cards from her fan and slaps them face up on the oilcloth, and sure enough she has a pair – two threes, hearts and spades.

Barbara is always fooling them. She is the sharp one of the maids, and as unlike Mollie, her sister and elder by two years, as it's possible to be. Barbara is short, not more than five foot. She has a round, pimply face and small features; her eyes are grey and sly, her no-colour hair is scraped back from her forehead. Because of her sharpness and her grating and sarcastic remarks, her singing voice comes as a surprise. She sings 'Open the door, Richard' (her young man's name is Dick) and 'Give Me Five Minutes More' and 'I Surrender, Dear' very sweetly when she cleans the bathrooms and the stairs.

Mollie is perhaps two inches taller. She hasn't got a young man (which is strange because she is prettier than Barbara), and she hasn't got spots. Her dark hair waves and curls round her oval face; her cheeks are red, her eyes brown. Mollie's eyes fill easily with tears. A sad song, a baby in a pram, a bunch of primroses – and Mollie's eyes brim and she dabs them with a drenched handkerchief.

More embarrassing even than her tears is her habit of hugging and kissing them. Each time they come to stay at Grandmother's house, she is waiting in the hall when they arrive – hands clasped together, lips parted, face pink and radiant in its halo of curls. Oooh, aren't they lovely, aren't they grand, Mollie says in a sort of gasp; and she grabs them in turn and lifts them off the ground and covers their eyes, their cheeks, their mouths, with kisses and tears. She presses their faces to her bosom so they can't breathe; she murmurs Darling, Sweetheart, My Love into their hair. It is terrible, but there is no way of avoiding it.

Even though experience has taught them she is not to be trusted, they prefer Barbara and Barbara's style. She takes no part in the welcome ceremony. If she happens to be in the hall, she stands on her own by the stairs, hand on hip, tapping a black shoe and looking the other way. When she does look at them, her expression is cool; if she does speak, her words are brief and uncomplimentary:

What a great fat thing you are now, Lucy – couldn't get me arms round you if I wanted. Which I don't. Look at Alice, dressed up to kill. Quite the little London lady, aren't we – eh?

Barbara calls them Southern Spivs and Foreigners. She mimics the way they pronounce bath and path. When she's in a bate she says they're toffee-nosed. If either of them unthinkingly begins a sentence 'I really think' or 'Actually, I', Barbara will pounce: Oh I *rarely* think, don't yoou? *A*ctually, my deah – and she blows smoke rings at the ceiling, transferring her cigarette from its normal position (between index finger and thumb) to the one (between index finger and second) film stars and nobs use. When Barbara mocks them, Mollie's eyes fill and she touches her sister's arm: Don't Barb – it's not their fault, poor loves – and then she turns to them and chats about her and Barb's mother who is a widow and

112

lives in a terraced cottage down by the railway line; or she asks about London, where she and Barb have never been. Is it much bigger than Liverpule? What are the shops like, like? Is there a Marshall's? Bigger than the one in Lord Street?

They do not love the maids, but they are fascinated by them, especially Barbara. They do not love their grandmother, whose house this is and has always seemed to be though their grandfather bought it, and though until two years ago he was alive and going daily on the train to his sack business in Bootle. When they think of him they think of his pipes and wiry hair and middle parting, his habit of changing red bedroom slippers for black shoes in the dining-room after breakfast; they remember the way he – sitting at the head of the table beneath his boardroom likeness on the wall – ate that breakfast; chomping so hard they feared he might dislocate his jaw, while grease from his bacon and egg ran in shiny, interesting rivulets down his navy blue chin; blotting his chin with a stiff-as-card napkin, before chomping his toast and marmalade. Grandfather left early and returned late, and in the evenings and at weekends was protected from them by Grandmother (Don't disturb your Grandfather!) so they never saw much of him at all. Grandfather is dead, and they miss him, but they feel he can't have gone far: his check caps and smelly mackintoshes – so long they almost graze the slopped water from the dogs' drinking bowls on the tiled floor – still hang in the porch; his walking sticks and canes and golf clubs still clutter the stick rack.

They do not love their grandmother. There is only one person in her house they love: Edie, who came to look after their own mother when she was a baby and never got away. Edie is housekeeper, cook (since Kate left in a huff), chauffeur (since Thomas left in the war) and slave to Grandmother's whims. And she does everything for them. She washes and irons their clothes, she gets them up and puts them to bed. She takes them on the train to the cinema in Southport and to the theatre in Liverpool. She drives them to the Village and buys them sweets and comics and drawing paper and pencils; she walks them to the shore, and on the

113

endless journey back (between grey asparagus fields and wind-bitten pines), she carries their wet bathing things. She reads to them by the hour, although they are, as Grandmother says, great girls of eight and nearly ten and can read for themselves. When she dozes off, which she always does (her head falls on her chest, her spectacles mist up, she snores), they prod her awake and make her carry on.

Edie is tall and big-boned. She has a high, receding forehead, a big nose, big eyes – very dark brown behind her specs – a big mouth and big teeth. Her hands (the gloves they gave her one Christmas wouldn't pull on at all) and feet are man-sized, her bosom a pillow whose weight of feathers collects just above the waist. Edie wears pale silky blouses with tucks and pleated fronts and little collars, under which she pins a cameo or pearl tie-pin. Even when the weather's boiling, she wears a cardigan – voluminous, and buttoned below the pillow with three buttons. She wears loose skirts of soft wool and elasticated knickers that reach almost to the knee; thick stockings, through which, when she sits down (not often, she's always on the go) they can see the ridge of her support bandages. For Church and for expeditions to Town, Edie wears a hat – felt, with a wide brim and a bow at the side, secured by a hat pin. Surprisingly for an unfrivolous person, she loves hats. Sometimes she says to them: Do you like my new hat, dears? and they stand on tiptoe and examine it from all sides and say, Yes we do, but the new hat is the same as her old one, the same as all her other hats. When Edie wakes them in the morning she wears her old dressing-gown, which is a man's and thick and heavy as a carpet.

Edie never alters – how old is Edie? If they ask, she is ninety-nine next birthday, dear. Has Edie ever been in love? That would be telling, Duck. Edie does everything that servants do, but she is not a servant. She never has a day off. Also, she calls Grandmother Mummy, though she is not Grandmother's daughter, and not young enough to be. Grandmother calls Edie Nurse, a cold starched title that does not suit her, and treats her badly, bullying her at mealtimes and bossing her. Edie never answers back. While Grandmother's blows fall, she sits in silence, staring out through the thick glass of her spectacles and the window, or at her plate. If Lucy asks, Why is Granny so horrible to you? Edie says, Oh I don't know, Duck – she has her problems, I daresay, and changes the subject and gets out the ironing board.

Edie gossips about no one, has no small talk, keeps her thoughts to herself. She talks to the cocker spaniels, she calls them Old Dear, Old Darling, Old Lady while she defleas their coats and untangles their ears with a steel comb. After breakfast she feeds the spaniels with Radio malt kept for that purpose in the nursery on a curtained-off shelf. The malt falls from the spoon on to the first finger of Edie's left hand, she spins the spoon and the malt winds round the finger like a bandage. The dogs have a finger of malt each. With their tongues they pull and tug at the bandage, and the malt enters their mouths in long strings, like rubber bands. This happens every morning, after bedmaking, after going to the lavatory, and it is very interesting to watch.

It is now, just about now, that Grandmother comes to the nursery. She huffs and puffs through the door; she blows out her cheeks; she sits heavily in the rocking chair; she leans back and rocks; she stares around her in disapproval. She has come to order the shopping. Edie makes a list and Grandmother huffs and puffs and blows out her cheeks. Grandmother is ugly and her ugliness is made worse by all the huffing and puffing. Does she know she does it? If she could see herself, would she? She leans back in her chair and crosses and recrosses her legs, examining her ankles, twisting them round. She is proud of her ankles and her calves and her small feet. Her clothes cupboard contains hundreds of pairs of shoes, all from Raynes, all new-looking, all with tissue paper crushed into their toes. Grandmother judges people by their extremities. If asked her opinion of so-and-so, she will answer: Pretty ankles – i.e. Yes – or Ugly calves – i.e. No. It is as well she doesn't judge people by their stomachs. Her own is a barrel that gurgles and heaves as she rocks.

What are the girls going to do today, Nurse? Grandmother asks Edie, puffing and rocking. If she addresses them directly, it's You girls, if indirectly, The girls. Grandmother doesn't like girls. Men (sons-in-law are the exception) are gods, boys heroes, girls nothing and good for nothing. Girls have no brains, no talents, no virtues. Grandmother has two sons and four daughters, four grandsons and six grand-daughters, but you would never guess this from the snapshots of curly-headed heroes she keeps by her bed, or from the studio portraits of uniformed gods that stand on the piano. Grandmother doesn't conceal her prejudice or bother to defend it. Example: Alice and Lucy are good at drawing and painting; they do it all the time, they've won prizes, they fill a drawing book a week. If they take their drawing books to Grandmother for her inspection, she flips the pages without looking or stopping. Handing them back without comment, she then praises the efforts of their cousin Robert who, as everyone knows, can't draw for toffee. (Once, when their drawing books were full, and Edie busy in the kitchen, they went to Grandmother and asked her for threepence each for a new one; and Grandmother said, Why should I pay out good money for your scribbles? and turned on her Raynes high heel.)

Example 2: On one occasion, when Robert – at that time a shaven-headed thug of six – was over for tea, he hit Alice on the head with one of Grandfather's golf clubs he'd taken from the porch. The blow was intentional; it knocked Alice out and produced a large bump on her temple, but it was Robert who cried. While Alice was left for dead (until Edie came, summoned from the fruit cage by Lucy), Grandmother took the bellowing hero on to her lap and kissed and comforted him and fed him liquorice allsorts from a paper bag.

Grandmother must, presumably, have been a girl herself once. So why doesn't she like girls?

When Grandmother asks Edie in that snide way (which implies they are lazy good-for-nothings) what the girls are going to do today, they want to ask: What are *you* going to do today, Granny?

They know what they will be doing. Shopping with Edie, drawing, reading (the bound volumes of *Little Folks* and *The Girls' Own Annual*; the Red, Green and Violet Fairy Books); walking the dogs; quick-stepping to Geraldo and Jack Payne and Roy Fox (on the radiogram in the Big Room); lining up lead soldiers and lead nurses and stretcher bearers; staging a drama in the toy theatre (a model of the Liverpool Playhouse, with working lights and scenery and an orchestra pit): staging a drama in the dolls' house (a model of Grandmother's house, even to the motor cars in the garage and the petrol pump outside it); dressing up – as pirates (clothes and jewels from the dressing up chest on the landing); building card houses and brick houses; playing snakes and ladders and ludo (with Edie); playing Old Maid (with the maids). And in summer the list is longer. In summer they can add riding the cranky bikes that belonged to their aunts when they were young; knocking up on the red tennis court; paddling and bathing in the sea. (Or, if the sea is too far out, which it very often is – a thin smear between the sand and the sky – shrimping in pools on the ribbed sand). They will be plunging their hands for frogs in any one of five lily ponds; jumping off the stone balls that surmount the terrace wall; eating their way through hot houses and vegetable gardens and plum orchards. They know what they will be doing. What will Grandmother be doing?

Grandmother will be sitting and rocking, if not in the nursery upstairs, in the drawing-room downstairs, if not in the drawing-room, in the morning-room, if not in the morning-room, in the summer house. Or, should the day be really hot and sunny, she will be found under the awning of the swing seat on the terrace, swinging and perhaps reading. (And that – apart from loading the bird-table and feeding the red squirrels and the goldfish – is all Grandmother seems to do.) When Grandmother reads, she holds the book like a shield in front of her face and moves her head from side to side and mutters the words aloud. She reads the same books over and over again – *A Little Green World* is the title of one of them. As Edie coaxes the tea trolley over the crazy paving (the

maids are off duty till six) and unstacks the brown-spotty tea
service cups and plates, Grandmother goes on reading. Alice drags
a teak table to the swing seat, Lucy jumps to with a cup of tea and a
plate of sandwiches, but Grandmother doesn't say thank you. She
stretches a hand for a sandwich without looking up from the page,
and goes on muttering. Grandmother is rude.

Grandmother is mad. It must be madness that brings her, in
corsets and petticoat, into the spare room where they sleep. (They
don't sleep; they lie awake till early light, reading and discussing
the madness of Grandmother.) She comes at bedtime, or after
lunch when they are resting on their beds. She huffs into the room
and leans against the clothes cupboard, or on her elbows over the
mahogany foot of the nearest bed. She massages the back of her left
hand with the fingertips of her right. Her shoulders are grooved
with pink shoulder straps, three or four to each shoulder. Edie
comes to the spare room to tuck them up (they lock their arms
round her neck; they won't let her go) and draw back their
curtains in the morning; to say, Sweet dreams, darlings, or Time
to get up, Lucy old duck; Edie comes to take away their dirty
clothes or bring them clean ones, to help them make their beds.
Grandmother comes for one purpose only: to tell lies about her
eldest daughter (their mother) and her daughter's husband (their
father). Grandmother tells them their mother is a hussy and
irresponsible; that she has abandoned them and gone off to
America because she does not love them and can't be bothered to
look after them. She says their father is a fortune hunter who
married their mother for her money; that he is idle; that he is dull;
that he is too clever by half; that there is bad blood in his family;
and that she could tell them a thing or two . . . .

If they lie still and shut their eyes and ears and say nothing, she
eventually goes away, banging the door behind her. But she is
always back. They count to twenty and watch the doorknob and it
turns, and there she is again, in the doorway, huffing. And another
thing – she begins, and goes on and on and on. She may leave and
return half-a-dozen times to tell more and worse lies about their

parents; or she may stand huffing but without speaking, just inside the door, one hand on the doorknob. If one of them (Lucy is the braver) sits up and shouts, How dare you say such wicked lies about our parents? How dare you? Why do you do it? Why? Grandmother closes her puffy eyes and smiles a secret, horrible smile. Or she shakes her fist at them and turns on her heel.

Can witches ever be fat? If so, Grandmother is a witch. Her loathing of cats, which amounts almost to fear (she will not have one in the house; the stray kitten Lucy found on the shore was banished within the hour), would seem to discount this, but there's a tiger on the wall of the main staircase, and a leopard stretched out on the carpet in the hall. And the terrace reeks of catmint, it grows between the paving and in every crevice of the wall. In any case, Grandmother does have a familiar of sorts – a Maltese terrier called Clarence. Clarence is a shivering whingeing piece of fluff, but the worst aspect of him is his smell. He smells, he stinks, of wee. This is because, when he widdles, he balances on both front legs in a handstand, so that his body and back legs go vertically into the air. Naturally the wee runs down his stomach, and as he wees a lot his underside is permanently yellow. Grandmother doesn't seem to notice the stain or the smell, or the dark and damp twist of hair at the end of his thing. She keeps him with her, on her lap in a rocking chair, or nestled beside her in the cushions of the swing seat. She hand-feeds him his dinner, a sickening mess of boiled rabbit and chicken and sodden, baked bread. He is fussy, of course, and shivers and turns his nose away, and she has to coax and beg him. If he dares to escape, she huffs from room to room looking and calling: Clarrie, Clarrie, Clarrie, come to Mother, precious boy.

Grandmother has no taste. She worships the disgusting Clarence and ignores the spaniels who, if anyone leaves a gate open, risk no dinner and a beating to spend the day rabbiting in the pinewoods beyond the golf course.

Grandmother has no taste, but she is always talking about Taste. Taste is to do with shoes and dress stuffs, and also with carpets and curtains and chair covers. Grandmother is houseproud, she likes everything just so, and she has a thing about loose covers. Loose covers? Loose covers may be all right in their way, nothing wrong with loose covers, but not something to get worked up about. Grandmother gets very worked up about them. She leans back in the drawing-room sofa (blue-grey roses, green leaves on a white ground) and strokes its loose-covered arm. Come here, girls, she says, and feel these beeauuutiful loose covers – She does the same thing with curtains – flowered chintz in every room of Grandmother's house. Look, girls, she says, holding them out like skirts from the window, They're lined and interlined, beeauutifully made. You'll go a long way before you see curtains as beautiful as these. Or she bends down (not an easy feat for her) and pats the carpet. Puuure wool Wilton, she says. Come and feel it girls, puure puure wool . . . Grandmother's obsession brings her into the nursery where they are drawing or playing ludo, where Edie is washing their pants in the marble basin beside the window. She huffs and puffs through the door with a roll of something under her arm, and unravels it on to their drawing books or the ludo board. This material is very expensive, she declares, holding a corner of it to her cheek. Look at it, girls, feel it. (She makes them pinch and stroke it). One day – she says with an important pause – You may be lucky enough to own material of this quality . . . After she's gone (very suddenly and huffily, bored perhaps with their lack of enthusiasm), Lucy will lift a corner of the tablecloth and hold it to her cheek. Look at this, girls, she'll says, it's puure, puure gingham. One day you may be lucky enough to own . . . Very naughty, Duck, Edie says, straightening up from the basin, her arms soapy to the elbows. *Very* naughty. But when they shriek and roll around and clutch themselves, Edie laughs too. There's no malice in Edie's laughter. It's the best noise in the world.

Grandmother is unfair. Don't tell tales, she says, should they complain that one of their hero cousins (over for tea) has pinched or punched or hit them on the head with a croquet mallet. But should the hero tell tales on them, they're sent supperless to the spare room. That'll teach you to bully your dear little cousin, Grandmother says. It's not fair, they grumble, but Grandmother has an answer to everything. Life isn't fair, she says. Whoever said it was?

Grandmother breaks all the rules, the rules for living and behaviour that she has laid down. You can't get out of life what you don't put in, she's always telling them, but what does she put in, exactly? Let your meat stop your mouth, she orders when they chatter at lunch, yet she herself talks incessantly, and with her mouth full, a muttered monologue of complaint, addressed to everyone and no one. Sitting in silence while Grandmother mutters on, they may catch Barbara's eye (the maids wait at table and between courses stand either side the fireplace) and if they do, Barbara will wink and pull faces at them. When Grandmother isn't looking, she pulls faces at Grandmother, and sticks her tongue out before resuming a demure posture, eyes cast down, hands folded on her apron.

Grandmother is superstitious. Stop that Cornishman drowning! she barks if anyone accidentally knocks a glass at table; and the culprit hastily touches the rim to silence the ring and save the Cornishman from his fate.

Grandmother is mean. Get me a quarter of pontefract cakes and a quarter of liquorice allsorts, will you, Nurse, she orders as they leave for the village, but she keeps her sweet ration in her bedroom and never shares it.

Once a week Grandmother accompanies them on the shopping trip. She wears a hat (velour, veiled) and sits in the passenger seat of the Hillman with a basket of empty cider bottles on her knee. Stop at Dean's, Nurse, she orders, which is where Edie is going anyway. At Dean's, which is the grocers, Edie gets out and they get out, and Grandmother stays in the car with her basket. Dean's smells of bacon and coffee. Edie stands at the counter reading out her list, and Mrs Dean finds all the items from the shelves and licks her pencil to make it blacker and writes everything down in the invoice book. As soon as Edie enters the shop, Mr Dean peers

121

through the window, and if he sees Grandmother in the car he drops whatever he's doing and abandons whoever he's serving and hurries out to her. Grandmother winds down the window and Mr Dean bows before her, his hands clasped to the chest of his green button-through overall. How are you today, Mrs Moss? he says, and Grandmother's puffy face explodes in smiles. She nods and chats and tosses her head. She laughs in a girlish way. This performance is repeated everywhere they go. Grandmother stays in the car, and Mr Taylor, Mr Cross, Mr Bower and Mr Darbyshire all leave their businesses to pay court to her. And she is charming to them all.

Only at the wine merchants is this pattern broken. Rimmer's is not in the High Street, and does not look like a shop. It's a tall brick house in an ordinary road of tall brick houses. The Hillman jerks to a halt outside the gate, and Edie goes round and opens the passenger door for Grandmother, and then Grandmother, on her own with the basket, huffs and puffs up the path and the steps and vanishes through the front door. They wait in the car for what feels like an hour (Edie taps the steering wheel and looks at her watch), and eventually Grandmother reappears all smiles, with Mr Rimmer beside her carrying the basket which is heavy now because the cider bottles are full.

Shopping is quicker when Grandmother doesn't come, and more enjoyable. They can chew their way from shop to shop because Edie buys them peppermint lumps at Darbyshires, and they are treated like royalty everywhere they go. These are Mrs Moss's little granddaughters from the big house, Mrs Dean or Mrs Darbyshire will announce to the other customers, and the other customers gasp and stare and pass admiring remarks, as though Alice and Lucy were the Princesses Elizabeth and Margaret Rose.

Why is Grandmother so important? Is it because she was married to Grandfather, who was a very rich man? Or because her house is so large? It is enormous, but there are other large houses in that very long road. It does have special features: it is the only one with a hard tennis court and orchards; and it is the nearest to the shore. Outside Grandmother's gate the metalled road gives up and a flatly cobbled, cindered and sandy track takes over. Day-trippers from Liverpool to the sea stop here, and put down their spades and nets and hoist themselves on to the wall or the stone balls of the gateposts to get a view – for Grandmother's garden is the most splendid for miles. If the gate is, unusually, open, the trippers may even venture inside and stand on the white gravel and gaze at the blazing borders and ornamental trees and striped lawns, at the terrace where the lady of the house and her family are (self-consciously, for they feel like a tableau) having tea. Shut the gate now, girls, Grandmother orders when the day-trippers at last back out of the drive, still gazing and exclaiming. (Surprisingly, Grandmother never tells the trippers to go away. She calls out Good afternoon, and waves graciously from the swing seat and beams at them from under her sun hat).

Not many invited visitors come to Grandmother's house. Perhaps it's because she doesn't like women that Grandmother has so few friends. Once in a blue moon a visitor does come (for tea always, never for lunch or dinner), but whatever it is between them, it doesn't seem like friendship. The visitor is always very polite to Grandmother and agrees with everything she says in a way friends generally don't, and calls her Mrs Moss and not Dilys, which is Grandmother's first name.

Is Grandmother lonely? Does she miss the time (the photograph albums in the morning room record) when the terrace steps were ranked with young men waving cricket bats, and girls with tennis racquets and frizzy perms (can that one in the eyeshade be their mother?), when the drive was chock-a-block with Morgans and MGs?

Does she miss her children after all?

Does she, after all, miss Grandfather?

Sometimes when they come across Grandmother rocking and muttering, they find the muttering is weeping. If they can, they creep away before she's seen them – if not, she collars them. Come here darlings, she says – darling a word normally reserved for

123

grandsons and for Clarence. She makes them sit at her knee. She imprisons their hands. She tells them their Grandfather was a great and good man, a wonderful man, a brilliant man. He was the best husband, the best father, the best grandfather who ever lived. Their grandfather was – they must remember this, they must never forget it – a saint. There aren't many saints in this world, but he was one of them. A saint, do they understand? Their grandfather was a SAINT.

What is all this? Grandfather was a kind man, kind to them when they saw him, kind to Grandmother so far as they could tell; and his children had all loved him, so he must have been kind to them. He was hard-working and good at cricket, and he had an interesting way of chomping his bacon and egg and talking while chewing his pipe. But they'd known him to lose his temper, and he sometimes made unsaintly remarks about Jews and Roman Catholics. Does Grandmother believe what she says? Does she believe they will believe it? Can it be she's forgotten how she treated Grandfather after his stroke? After his stroke Grandfather couldn't talk or feed himself or shave. He dribbled and coughed and his nose ran. Long strings of saliva fell unchecked down his shirt or pyjama jacket; if he leaned forward they collected in his lap. It must have been terrible for Grandfather, who'd always taken pride in his appearance, and who not long ago had been bowling to his grandsons and running to the net to smash a volley, but Grandmother mocked and jeered. While he sat slumped in his wheelchair, his eyes sunk and staring, she talked about him as though he wasn't there. Give it a rest, Mummy, Edie would say, very sharply for her. Leave Daddy alone. Let him be. But Grandmother would go on and on. What does it matter? she'd say, he's only a carcass. What does it matter?

Grandfather couldn't speak, or feed himself, or wash or go to the lavatory – but could he hear? What if he could understand? They discuss this possibility in bed at night, in the spare room; they decide that Grandmother is at her most awful when she sanctifies Grandfather. Of all her moods, this one, in which no word of remorse or regret ever interrupts the tearful listing of his virtues, is the worst.

When they can escape her, they run (through the hall, down the passage, past the pantry and the storeroom, through the kitchen) to the maids' sitting-room, a place where Grandmother almost never goes.

The maids' sitting-room smells of smoke and armpits. The smoke of a million Wills' Whiffs and Woodbines has tanned the once-cream walls and ceiling and worked its way into the uncut moquette of the sofa and the stringy rug that lies on the lino in front of the gas fire. To step into this room, to sit on the smoked sofa and lean elbows on the oilclothed table top, is to enter a different house. It is dingily lit (by a cone-shaped enamel light, dangling from a chancy flex); bereft of ornament (two plaster Alsations, merely, and an oak half-moon clock on the shelf above the fire); devoid of comfort (apart from the sofa, two hard kitchen chairs). The room is an odd shape, triangular, and has only one, very small, window, too high up to see out of and always closed.

The room is dangerous. Grandmother may not come here, but when Barbara shuts the door they risk, they are sure, never returning to Edie and safety again. The conversation is dangerous. As Barbara, fag hanging from her mouth, deals the cards – so old and smoked they stick together when she tries to shuffle them – as they pick them up and sort them into suits, she gossips about Grandmother. Mrs M. is a silly old cow, Barbara says, a right bitch, and what she pays her and Mollie is laffable, not mind you that she's laffing. Come here, Clarrie, Barbara says in Grandmother's voice – and she gets up and hunts round the room and under the table for Clarence, walking bow-legged like Grandmother, bending down and patting the inside of her right knee, as Grandmother does: Come to mother, darling, precious boykin . . . . (They don't like Grandmother; they fear her and talk about her in bed in the spare room. So why does Barbara's performance – which is accurate and very funny – make them anxious?)

When Barbara has said all she has to say on the subject of Grandmother, they talk Smut. Barbara is the leader, but they all do it, even Mollie, though it makes her more than usually pink-faced. Through round after round of Old Maid (invariably Alice) and Rumblebelly and Strip Jack Naked and Seven of Diamonds and Snap, they talk of bosoms and bottoms, bras and knickers, lavs and chamber pots. Eyes, nose, mouth and chin, Barbara says, touching these features with a small grey hand, all the way down to Uncle Jim (she sticks the hand between her legs); Uncle Jim makes lemonade (Pssssssssss – to indicate wee), round the corner (hand goes round the back, to Barbara's bottom) chocolate's made (plop plop plop plop – to indicate number twos). Red, white and blue, Dirty Kangaroo, went behind the dustbin, and did his number two (fart noises; more plops). My Uncle Billy had a ten foot willy, he showed it to the lady next door – Eee, don't, Barb, Mollie interrupts, you musn't, they're too young.

When Barbara leans across the table to tweak a card from Lucy, her underarm smell fills the room. They know she washes, they've seen her in the maids' bathroom stripped to the waist, bent over the tiny corner basin. She soaps herself with sour yellow soap. Under each arm is a pelt of black fur, like the false moustaches in the dressing-up chest on the landing. Grown-up women don't put soap on their faces, they use Ardena Deep Cleansing Cream, but Barbara works the yellow bar between her hands and lathers her face into bubbles all over, screwing her eyes tight and blowing out her cheeks as though she were inflating a balloon. If invited, they follow her along the passage to the maids' bedroom and watch her change. (The maids wear green dresses and white aprons in day time; black dresses with frillier aprons and cuffs and caps in the evening). The rooms in Grandmother's house are painted cream or pastel shades of blue or grey, but the maids' bedroom is wallpapered with roses, red, yellow and blue, giant blooms, and the door and skirtings are an outdoor green. It's a dark room because the one window looks on to the wash-house wall, and it smells – of smoke and of the contents of the chamber pots, one under each brass bed. (Once, when Alice, for some reason in the maids' bedroom without Lucy, caught sight of Barbara's po and smelt its sickly-sweetish smell, its contents were red – like water beetroot's boiled in, she told Lucy afterwards: Perhaps Barbara had cut her bottom? Lucy suggested.)

The maids wear black stockings in the evening when they change, but in daytime, even in winter, their legs are bare and sore-looking, descending to red ankles and black lace-up shoes. Their legs are bare when they go off on their bikes on Thursday afternoons. In winter they ride away in belted coats and headscarves and high-heeled shoes; in summer they put on shiny rayon dresses which have shoulder pads and ruched sleeves, and they squeeze their feet into tiny sling-backs with peep toes. Grandmother doesn't allow make-up on duty, but on Thursday afternoons when they pedal off, their eyebrows are black and arched, their eyelids mauvey purple, their mouths a hard dark red.

Where do the maids go on Thursday afternoons? MYOB, Barbara says, as she and Mollie wheel their bikes down the path between the tennis court and the holly hedge to the back gate. To see a man about a dog, she says, unlatching the gate, or, Wouldn't you like to know?

But one time when they ask, Mollie says they can come next time, if they like; they'll go shopping in the High Street, and then have tea at home. Our mother's heard a lot about you two, she says. Better ask your Grandma, Barb calls over her shoulder, Better ask Mrs M.

They won't ask Grandmother, they'll ask Edie. I don't see why not, Duck, Edie says, If you behave yourselves.

Grandmother hears about it, of course. What do you want to do that for? she asks, puffing out her cheeks. It isn't suitable. Gentlefolk don't shop in the afternoon.

Later in the week Grandmother comes to the spare room and leans over the end of Alice's bed. Behind her on the wall, muddy clouds gather above a horse-drawn plough. You can't go on your bicycles, anyway, she says, as though adding to a conversation that has just taken place. It's too far and too dangerous, you'll have to walk.

What's all this? They ride their bikes every day, up Larkhill Lane as far as the Army Camp, along College Avenue, down Shireburn Road, all over the place and she never asks questions. Bike riding has never been dangerous before. But Grandmother won't listen to their pleas or change her mind. Don't go, then, she says. Take it or leave it; walk or don't go.

Next Thursday they're dressed in cotton frocks and cardigans, ankle socks and sandals. Let's have a look at you, Barbara says. Well . . . and Mollie squeezes the breath out of them and says, Aren't they lovely, aren't they grand? It's a hot day, and a long walk to the Village, which is not a village like the ones at home are – set among fields with a pub and a shop and a school and a church. The Village is mile upon mile of criss-crossing roads of shiny brick houses, in the middle of which is a High Street of shops. By the time they get there, the maids are wilting in their rayon, and they've got blisters on their heels because their socks have gone to sleep in their sandals.

What happens next, whatever it is, they will try to make sense of in the spare room tonight, and tomorrow night, and weeks of nights to come. What happens, what happened (or did not happen – but it was the same for both of them) was this: They were in the High Street, but it was not the High Street they knew. No, it had to be the High Street they knew, because there at the end of it was the Post Office with its clock and chain railing.

Try again. They were in the High Street they knew, but the shops were not the same shops. The shops they visit daily with Edie were not there; had vanished; did not exist. In their place were other shops that Barbara and Mollie knew well and kept popping into – for knitting wool; for a 'a pound of tripe for our mother, Jack love;' for black stockings; for 'necessaries'; for a tired-looking cabbage.

Everywhere they went, the shopkeepers greeted the maids with: 'Lo Barb love, is yer fellar still at sea, then? or How's my Mollie?

Be a love and take this packet of lard, yer Mam left it behind last Tuesday – while they were ignored. Even when Barb – in answer to a baker they'd never seen before's, You've bin keeping these kids very quiet, I must say – said, They're Mrs M.'s grandchildren from the big house, no one seemed interested. The baker said, Oh yeh, without looking up, and put five buns in a paper bag and swung the bag by the corners and handed it to Barb.

Where were they? Outside, the pavement, the shops, the cherry trees, the parked bicycles and prams, swam in the heat. They looked at each other in panic.

Where were they? Lucy tugged Barbara's arm. Where are we?

We're in the High Street, that's where, don't be daft, Barbara said.

They're hot, poor loves, Mollie said, they'll be wanting an ice.

There is only one place for ices – Darbyshires, where Edie buys their drawing books and peppermint lumps, and the pontefract cakes Grandmother never shares. Mrs Darbyshire will be pleased to see them. They will be safe in Darbyshires.

This way, Barbara said. A blistered door shimmered before them. She pushed it open and a bell jangled. They waited in the dark till a woman in hair curlers came out of the back and leant her bosom on the counter. Two wafers, two cones, Marge, Barbara said. And don't forget me Woodbines –

Out on the pavement the margarine ices turned to sticky rivers that trickled over their wrists. Alice can't eat vanilla I'm afraid, Lucy said to Barb before Alice could stop her. It makes her sick. Oh, my lady can't eat vanilla – Barbara dropped a curtsey – Well, there's some of us as can – and she took the cornet from Alice's hand and finished it off with three sharp bites.

Where are they? Why isn't Edie here? Why doesn't she save them? Where *are* they?

They are in an alleyway between high brick walls.

One minute they were in the High Street, the maids' High Street, and the next they were following Barb through a brick arch, into an alleyway. There is no brick arch, and no alleyway in

Edie's High Street.

Nearly there now loves, Mollie said, as the walls crumbled to iron railings and spiky grass, through which they could see snippets of back gardens and washing-lines and the backs of dark houses. Our mother'll give us a nice cup of tea. Barb's and Mollie's mother will give them a nice cup of tea, and they will be able to go to the lavatory. Lucy was already crossing her legs.

In front of them the alley ended in a bank of pale grasses, dotted with willow trees and rising steeply to the railway line. Just before they reached it, Barbara opened a gate on the right, and they followed her up a brick path.

A witch was sitting on the doorstep, shelling peas into a basin. Her knees were wide apart and the tin basin, full of peas, rested between them on the step. She was bent forward and her long hair fell in front of her face and over her knotted arms. The step, her worn skirt and the path at her feet were littered with pea pods.

'Lo Mum, Barbara shouted above the noise of a train, rattling past on the embankment. How's tricks, our Mother? The witch parted her hair, and when she saw them she thew back her head and cackled. She had no teeth. Her mouth was a black cave. She was a hundred-years old. So these are Mrs M.'s girls, she whispered in a gummy lisp, and she stretched out her arms and pulled them to her as Mollie does, and kissed and squeezed them as Mollie kisses and squeezes them, and her hair went in their mouths and noses. Then she pushed them away and poked their stomachs with a knobby finger. Fat, she said, pinching Lucy's arm above the elbow. Fat, both of them. Fat as butter. And the black cave opened again and she laughed and laughed and laughed.

Never again, Barbara said on the endless walk back to Grandmother's house, Never again, Misses High-and-Mighty. Too grand to say a word to our mother. Not a peep, not a smile, not a please or a thank you out of the pair of you.

But it wasn't their fault they couldn't speak or eat, or drink their tea. The witch had cast a spell on them; she'd turned them to stone. It wasn't their fault. They looked at Mollie, but Mollie, who always defends them, pursed her mouth and said nothing.

On the way back Lucy wet her knickers (and her legs and her socks and her sandals). Having been turned to stone she couldn't, of course, follow Barbara to the wooden hut at the end of the witch's garden.

Grandmother was in the swing seat when they turned in the drive. Clarence yapped and whined, but Grandmother didn't look up as they climbed the terrace steps; she went on puffing and muttering and turning the pages. At the entrance to the porch the maids left them without saying goodbye, and went round the side of the terrace and down the side steps – past the hen run and the first vegetable garden – to the back door.

Did you have a nice time, dears? Edie said when they ran at her. They wanted to tell her, but they couldn't. What could they tell?

Barbara sent them to Coventry for a fortnight. If they met her on the stairs she looked the other way and hummed under her breath. In the dining-room she stared through them or over the tops of their heads. Mollie didn't speak either, but she gazed at them sorrowfully, pink in the face.

It's months before they're invited to the maids' sitting-room to play cards. When they do, Barbara doesn't gossip about Grandmother, and she doesn't pretend to hunt for Clarence, and nobody talks smut. Alice had got the Queen – as per, Barbara says in a bored voice, blowing smoke rings at the ceiling; and she winks – at Mollie, not at them.

They spend less time with the maids now, more time with Edie, more time by themselves.

Most mornings they go shopping with Edie in the Hillman. They go to Taylor's and Cross's and Bower's, they go to Dean's and Darbyshire's. If Grandmother comes, she sits in the passenger seat with a basket of empties on her knee, and all the shopkeepers leave their customers to pay court to her.

As they follow Edie from shop to familiar shop, they fear that at any moment they will find themselves in that other High Street they visited with the maids; the street where there is a greengrocer

131

with tired vegetables, the blistered door of a tobacconist that sells ices and a brick arch that leads to a terraced cottage under the railway line.

Bad Taste

'Rinse please,' Mr Payne said. He removed the saliva ejector from Mrs Carter's mouth and gave the instrument tray a little push. It swung smoothly away.

'I shall need to see you again in about a month. Get the appointment book would you, Diane?'

While Mrs Carter rinsed and spat three times with pink mouthwash, Dennis Payne soaped his hands energetically and dried them on a paper towel which he crumpled and dropped into a pedal bin under the basin.

Mrs Carter was still stranded in the chair. He dabbed at the dribble on her chin with a pink tissue from the dispenser, unclipped her plastic bib, and then brought her back to earth with one press of the foot-pump.

Mrs Carter climbed awkwardly off the chair. She'd been coming to him for years and in all that time he'd never hurt her; but she was still a nervous patient, a fact that annoyed him although he never let it show.

'I want you to think about that crown,' he said as he helped her into her coat and as Diane hovered with the appointment book. 'Gold is undeniably expensive, but it should last for ever. And it won't notice, I promise you.'

At the door he shook hands heartily with Mrs Carter and stood smiling, his hand raised in salute, until she was halfway down the stairs and obscured from his view by the landing banisters.

It was his last appointment of the morning. Running late – two extractions, and then the Bronson boy to be fitted in with an abscess – meant only an hour for lunch, whereas he needed an hour and a half. In winter he drove home in the lunch hour, to a house called Heatherdene, a mile from the practice and from the centre of the town, up a steep, conifer-clad hill above the golf course. In summer, and if the weather was fine, he ate his lunch in the park. The notice on the iron gates said Pleasure Gardens, a name he liked for the picture it conjured of pretty women with parasols gliding along well-tended gravel, but could never bring himself to use. When it rained he went to the King's Head in the High Street for a pint of Courage and a Beef Wellington.

Today, the 14th of May, he decided on the park, even though the weather was unsettled and cold. He called in at Blake's to see if the Atco was ready and was told, 'Any day now, Sir': and then walked briskly over the railway-crossing towards the park gates.

The park was almost empty: no one on the paths and benches; no boats on the lake. Only one couple on the tennis courts, a disappointment for he enjoyed watching tennis, a game he'd once enjoyed playing. It cheered him to see healthy young people engaged in healthy activity, particularly when the majority of youth passed their days and nights in stupor on the steps of the Gaumont.

He walked down a pitted asphalt path between the tennis courts and a low privet hedge, beyond which lay the putting green where a boy in jeans and a leather jacket chased a boxless Hayter Senator that expelled a spray of fine green dust. He skirted the empty bandstand – roundabout without horses Donald had called it when he was small – and made for his usual bench. Before sitting, he tested the slats with the palm of his hand, and then covered a section of seat with the fashion pages of the *Telegraph*. For a long time he sat and stared out at the lake, a rectangle of white water and not unlike a giant swimming pool. Its only pretentions to naturalism were the two islands in the middle, but even these were of uniform size, shape and planting, and equi-distant from the two end banks. Later in the summer, the lake and its environs would be intolerable, with ducks having to dodge the fibreglass rowing boats that, despite a large prohibitive notice, behaved little better than bumper cars; but today the boats were imprisoned under the brick arch of the boat house, and the ducks had the water to themselves.

Dennis unwrapped his lunch. Sheila had given him a Scotch egg, home-made and misshapen, the sausagemeat already dissociating itself from a green albumen; two rounds of wholemeal sandwiches that discharged shredded lettuce hearts and salad cream and slabs of shot-silk ham; a can of Export ale and an apple. He rummaged in his lunch box for the tube of mustard that would make the Scotch egg palatable, and then turned his head to check that there was no one about whom he knew. There was always the fear that one of his patients might discover him with cheeks distorted by sponge cake, or with pastry crumbs on his trousers.

He ate half the Scotch egg and all but one of the sandwiches, then threw the leftovers to the rabble of mallard and pintails who shouted at him from the bank.

'Hallo, Mr Payne. I was sure it was you.' He'd got no further than the front page of the *Telegraph* when he was interrupted by a voice that sounded young and female and very close. He lowered his newspaper and saw a blurred vision in white, holding a tennis racket. He removed his reading spectacles, at the same time instinctively putting out a hand to cover his naked lunch box and its display of scrunched tinfoil and tattered greaseproof paper. In focus she became someone familiar, but he did not know who, and he felt at a disadvantage. Sitting down and having to look up was uncongenial to one who spent the greater part of his life standing up and looking down.

'I've been reading a lot about you in the *Gazette* lately,' the vision said. 'I'm sorry you've lost your battle.'

'Thank you.' Dennis knew what she referred to. He'd been fighting for three years to save the park, or a large chunk of it, from being turned into a Leisure and Sports Centre. A brick (this was his one success: they'd tried for concrete), glass and pantile complex was to swallow the putting green, three of the tennis courts – indoor courts would replace these – the Aileen Johnstone Memorial Garden and the Rock Walk. They had promised to move the marble drinking fountain to a new site by the lily pond, but he was sceptical about this. The bulldozers were due in September.

The vision smiled, and Dennis remembered who she was.

'How's the family, Elizabeth?' he could now ask. 'I saw your mother, just before Christmas I think it was.' He recalled the difficulty he'd had in fitting the bridge he'd made for Lady Spenser's upper molars. Elizabeth he hadn't seen for some time. She had large blue eyes and was prettier than he remembered. No, it wasn't prettiness, it was something more –

'I've been meaning to come and see you for ages,' she was saying. 'The trouble is, Mama always made the appointments, and now that I've left home I forget about things like dentists. I expect I've got a mouthful of holes.' He doubted this. Elizabeth had an excellent jaw and had never had any real problems with her teeth. Far fewer cavities than the average.

'As a matter of fact,' she went on, rather pink in the face, 'I've got a sore place under my tongue and a peculiar, well nasty, taste that comes and goes.' He was embarrassed by confidences that ought properly to be confined to the dental surgery. They had no place in the park.

'Telephone my nurse this afternoon,' he said, 'and I'll tell her to try and fit you in on a cancellation.' While they were talking he'd become gradually aware of a young man in shorts, leaning against the black trunk of a prunus and separated from them by a row of wintry flower-beds that lay, neatly dug over, awaiting bedding plants. Every so often the young man swiped at the grass with his tennis racket. Dennis turned his attention to the boathouse. Above a notice which read: 'LAKE PLEASURE GARDENS: Scale of Charges', hung a rusted electric clock whose hands pointed to ten to two. He folded his newspaper and got to his feet.

'Have you still got the Noah's Ark? I was always very keen on it,' Elizabeth said, skipping out of his way as he cleared the bench of debris.

'Yes, of course. You'll see it when you come for your appointment. Excuse me, Elizabeth, I must get back. Remember me to your mother. Don't forget to telephone this afternoon!' he called over his shoulder as he hurried away down a path lined with cherry trees whose pink, double blossoms were beginning to pale and drop. At each tree a rug of petals obliterated the asphalt, silencing his footsteps. As he turned right by the tennis club, he caught sight of Elizabeth. She was sitting on his bench with the young man and throwing bread to the ducks.

'Another potato, dear?' Sheila lifted the lid of the serving dish. She picked up the spoon to serve him.

'No. Thank you.'

'There's only plums for afters.'

'Plums will be very nice.'

They were having supper in the dining-room which, when the double doors were folded back, became an extension of the sitting-room. The room was cold, and the silences in their conversation were drowned by what seemed to Dennis unnaturally loud chewings and scrapings and swallowings. He put his napkin down on the table and got up to clear away. He did what he could to help Sheila with the chores. She'd had polio as a child and was lame as a result. She tired easily and had to rest on her bed for two hours every afternoon.

He put the dirty plates in the hatch and made two journeys to the table with pudding plates, a cut-glass bowl of stewed plums, and a heavy blue jug containing the custard they both preferred to cream.

'There was a letter from Donald today,' Sheila said as she ladled plums on to a plate. Donald was the miracle baby no less than five specialists had decided she couldn't have.

'Oh yes?' Dennis said cautiously. Sheila and Donald were thick as thieves; he felt habitually jealous and left out.

'He wonders whether we'd like to have the children for a fortnight when he and Jenny go to Spain in September.' There was a silence while he took this in and while Sheila attempted to pour tepid custard on to his plums. It was too thick and she had to help it out with a spoon.

'A fortnight sounds a long time.' He took the plate Sheila handed him. A glut of plums last autumn meant kilner jars full of them on all the larder shelves. Meant plum fool, plum crumble, plum jam, plum tart, plums and custard, every day forever and ever. He had recently considered cutting the tree down.

'Even with Mrs D. coming in,' he continued, 'I don't see how you'd manage.' It was not difficult to sound concerned. Donald's children were two and four and a handful. Jenny never said 'Don't' when little Alec jumped up and down on his grandparents' settee in his lace-ups. During their last visit, mercifully for only three days, little Natasha had refused to eat anything except bananas.

Sheila turned her head away to spit a plum stone into her spoon. Then she said: 'With you at home, dear, I'm sure we'll be able to cope.'

It was a direct hit, and below the plimsoll line (but perhaps, to be fair, she had not understood that he'd fleetingly forgotten that at the beginning of August he retired and would be at home all the time. When this happened, Payne, Branksome and Jefferies would become Branksome and Jefferies. And if the cocky young man who joined them six months ago, and who was still on trial – or was it the practice that was on trial? Hopwood made it seem so – proved any use, it would soon be Branksome, Jefferies and Hopwood). He felt something close to hatred for Donald who, at thirty-four, was successful already – two holidays abroad a year, and lots of breaks in-between – and who had an attractive and energetic wife, a physiotherapist. What made them think he'd want the kiddies to stay in the first weeks of his retirement?

'He has a nerve, I must say,' he said, getting up to make the coffee. Sheila would be upset by this remark, he knew; he avoided her eye. As he walked round the back of her chair, he noticed the crown of her head where light from the three-pronged oak candelabra formed a small halo. Her hair did not shine as hair should when light touches it. When she'd first started dyeing – tinting, she called it – her hair, he'd been pleased. But that was a long time ago. Now it seemed out of keeping with his own baldness and made her look hard, like the Duchess of Windsor, and common. Tarty, even. He would never tell her this. Even when she asked him, as she anxiously did from time to time: 'Do you think I should allow myself to go grey now?' he always reassured her: 'Not unless you want to.' He was not sure why he lied to her in these ways – as over the plums – whether it was out of kindness (for it might not be kind) or boredom.

'We needn't make up our minds yet about the children,' Sheila said when he returned with the coffee.

'No, of course we'll have them. Obviously.' He didn't want to talk about it anymore. Instead he said, rolling his napkin into a sausage and pushing it through a silver ring round whose desert a caravan of camels plodded: 'I saw Elizabeth Spenser in the park today. She'd been playing tennis, and came up and spoke to me while I was eating my lunch.'

'Is she the eldest? She must be eighteen or nineteen by now.'

'More like twenty, perhaps.' Still, Sheila, who'd never met Elizabeth and who knew few of his patients socially, wasn't far out. Throughout the years he'd tried to enliven her day by telling her selected gossip about his patients. It was not gossip so much as harmless news of births, marriages and deaths and, increasingly, of divorces and recouplings. Sheila had always appeared interested in this information, even grateful. She looked at him expectantly across the table, but he found he had nothing else he wanted to say about Elizabeth Spenser. Certainly not that, quite unaccountably, he'd thought about her several times in the course of the afternoon. She hadn't telephoned. He knew this because he'd checked the appointment book more than once before leaving the surgery.

She made her appointment the following morning, as he discovered at lunchtime. Tuesday, the twenty-second, at eleven thirty. He stared at this date on the page and at Miss Spencer, written in ballpoint in Diane's neat, backward sloping hand. There was something not quite right. It took him a minute to realize she'd spelt Spenser with a C instead of an S. It was not a mistake he could have made. He was meticulous on all matters concerning his patients, priding himself on his ability to store useful details about their lives and interests so that when some grey-flannelled (though latterly it had been jeans; everyone seemed to wear jeans these days, including the mothers), twelve-year-old came into the surgery, he was able to say, pumping hands vigorously: 'Hello Jeremy/Charles/Nicholas. How are you? And how are the model trains/computer games/stamps? I imagine you must be off to Marlborough/Eton/Radley any minute now?' This sort of thing, especially if the patient had problem teeth or was in any way nervous, was essential, a part of what poor old Neville Thompson – senior partner until his untimely death last October – had, perhaps tautologically, termed 'The Psychology of Confidence'.

It was raining hard. He'd been hoping to go to the park, not, he told himself, because there was any possibility Elizabeth would be on the tennis courts, or that he might find her seated on his bench alone with a book (where did she work? he wondered, if she did work. Where did she live, now that she'd left home? How did she spend her days? Her nights?) but because he needed the exercise.

In the crowded Monarch bar of the King's Head, he saw Joe Hincks having lunch with Mrs Hincks, and looked quickly away. Joe Hincks was a chartered quantity surveyor and his arch enemy on the council. The Leisure Centre was his baby. While Dennis and Brigadier Gough-Naylor had been campaigning to prevent it, Hincks had been organizing fund-raising activities to pay for it. For over a year now, the pavement outside the Town Hall had been taken up by a giant cardboard thermometer with a red needle that showed the target figure and the campaign success to date.

The slogan underneath read: 'It's your Leisure. Your future. Help pay for your Centre'. Inside, a spotlit architect's model of the projected building and the site, complete with miniature bathtub of water – the lake – stood on a rostrum flanked by hessian exhibition screens that displayed working drawings and plans and lists of fund-raising activities.

He had just forked in the last mouthful of chili con carne ('sorry dear, there's been a run on the Beef Wellington today'), and pushed some bruised lettuce and the remains of the pickle to the side of his plate, when Elizabeth walked in through the latticed oak doors, followed by someone who might very well be, indeed probably was, the fellow he'd seen her with in the park. He lowered his head at once, but by craning his neck a little could watch the two of them select a table, walk to it, and Elizabeth, who was wearing some sort of blue pyjamas, slide on to a bench seat with her back to the window. The young man removed a menu from an adjoining table and they conferred; he could see Elizabeth's finger travel up and down the card, hover and then rest at something. He edged round in his seat until they were no longer in sight and until he was fully facing the back of the bar, his eyes on a level with a shelf that supported a brass horse and trap, a laminated photograph of a girl in a track suit with 'I'd Love a Babycham' on her bosom, and rows of stem glasses with gold rims; and immediately Elizabeth's friend was beside him, one check, tweed arm resting on the counter, chubby fingers tapping.

'One glass of dry white, one pint of best, one cheddar ploughman's, one lasagne.' It was an educated voice. Well, it would be. That man knows Elizabeth, he thought. How well does he know Elizabeth?

'That'll be – ' Miriam behind the bar, whose prominent teeth pained Dennis each time he encountered them, was adding up on her note pad: 'Four pounds twenty altogether. Can you pay for the food now, sir, please?' Had Elizabeth chosen bread and cheese or lasagne? He wanted to know, but would not wait to find out.

He stared straight in front of him as he made for the exit and was almost at the door when he heard her, above the din of conversations and scraping plates and sudden hearty laughter, call out: 'Mr Payne!' and he turned his head. She was smiling at him and waving.

'See you next week, worse luck!' In answer, he raised his hand in a stiff little salute. As he headed for the door, he collided with Joe Hincks and Mrs Hincks, also on their way out, and had to apologize.

'Don't mind us, old chap. We can take it!' Hincks was infuriatingly jovial, almost avuncular.

When he opened his surgery door Diane, her back to him, was removing instruments from the sterilizer. Beside her stood Hopwood. His arms were folded across his chest and he half leaned against a glass-fronted cabinet that contained swabs and dressings. Dennis detected an air of easy intimacy between them he did not care for.

'I've been telling your nurse here,' Hopwood began, 'that it's high time you had some proper machinery. That old thing' – he uncrossed his arms and pointed at the sterilizer – 'looks like a toaster.' Diane arranged the steaming instruments on a tray and put her cheatle forceps on the draining board. With a practised tug at the finger ends she peeled off her cellophane gloves, at the same time touching the pedal bin with the toe of one black court shoe. The top flew up like the lid of a jack-in-the-box and snapped shut again, trapping one inflated and accusing finger in the rim.

'And I've told Mr Hopwood our sterilizer is fine, thank you very much.'

Dennis decided to ignore these exchanges. Hopwood had been consistently rude about the 'outmoded equipment' in the practice ever since he'd joined them, even going so far as to suggest, in his interview, that their method of mixing – in a mortar with a pestle – mercury and silver alloy, was potentially lethal. Unfortunately, he'd been by far the best qualified of the applicants they'd interviewed, and he didn't smoke. Once in, Hopwood had taken

144

no time at all to throw out the 'Dickensian' drill he'd inherited from Neville Thompson, and to instal an air rotar unit in its stead. Now each partner had one, a neat little Sirobox with a high-speed drill and a polisher that worked off compressed air. The new equipment had been expensive, and the fees had gone up as a result, which Dennis minded. He refused to admit to anyone that these innovations made life easier and dentistry more efficient, and he'd dug his toes in over the sterilizer which was perfectly adequate and would see him out, at least.

'What can I do for you?' he asked Hopwood, after a long silence during which he'd found himself a clean tunic and put it on.

'My X-Ray machine is on the blink – ' Hopwood's tone was languid ' – and I wondered, if you don't need it for an hour or so, if I might borrow yours?' There was, alas, no good enough reason for refusing. He did not need the X-Ray for his first two patients, and this was something that Diane, who could be relied on to do her homework thus far, knew quite well.

'Give Mr Hopwood a hand, would you, Diane?' He watched them wheel the cumbersome tripod to the door, Hopwood alternately tugging and pushing, Diane struggling with a tail of thick and shiny corkscrew flex that sprang out of her arms at every step. He did not offer to help them.

'Oh, Mr Payne . . . ' Diane, who was outside the door, popped her head round again. 'Mrs Payne phoned ten minutes ago. She said could you get a tin of Whiskas on your way home. She'd forgotten the corner shop shuts now on Tuesday afternoons. Rabbit flavour.' She failed to close the door behind her, and he could hear the Oralix's halting journey across the landing to Hopwood's room, Hopwood's muffled 'whoops' and then giggles. Were they laughing at him? He shut the door. In September, Whiskas, Dreft and Windolene, and whether or not Sheila had sufficient quantities, would be the most exigent problem he could expect to face. He looked round his room. It had been his refuge for thirty-five years, but in August it would be taken over by Mrs Jackson, the hygienist, who came in two days a week and who at present was making do with a cupboard-sized room downstairs. His patients appreciated – he knew this because they said so – the human touches in his surgery. The walls, for instance, were the palest coral pink. There were two Victorian watercolours, one above the fireplace, of a cottage with smoke spiralling from the thatch, a spreading oak tree and a collie dog; and the other, on the right of the door as you entered it, and on the only wall not taken up by cabinets and sinks and machinery, of two small children in straw bonnets gathering cowslips. At either end of the mantle-piece were propped photographs, a studio portrait of Donald aged five, sitting sideways to the camera on a cushion against a background of puffy clouds; and an unframed snapshot of Sheila, taken by himself. She was standing on the curved brick step outside the front door of Heatherdene, laughing and holding up Muffin, a tabby cat long since dead. Between the photographs, a pair of Staffordshire dalmations lay with their heads on their paws and eyed each other round a carriage clock that, despite regular visits to Mr Braine in Station Road, kept only idiosyncratic time. Dennis checked the entirely reliable Rolex – his one extravagance in a life of parsimony – on his wrist: the clock was running fifteen minutes fast.

A large, south-west facing window took up most of the wall opposite to the door. It showed, if you stood directly in front of it, as he now did, a square of mossy lawn edged with laurels and divided by a yellow gravel path, at the end of which a rose pergola, today sagged in the rain. For anyone in the dentist's chair, this vista was reduced to sky, telephone wire and the tops of three ragged Wellingtonias in the garden opposite. What the chair did provide was a panorama of the windowsill, and upon it, of his treasure – the Noah's Ark Elizabeth had mentioned in the park. Thirty-nine animals (fourteen pairs, one elephant missing) walked in perpetual orderly crocodile from right to left, to where the Ark stood with its gangplank down, and Mr and Mrs Noah on deck, to receive them. The Ark, a present to Dennis on his sixth birthday, had once been a bright scarlet and blue, but had darkened through the years so that now, although polished and handsome, it was no recognizable colour.

He got out a duster from a drawer in the wall unit. Since an elephant had gone missing ten years or so ago, and both antelopes had suffered fractures, no one but himself had been allowed to touch the animals except certain children who, he could tell, were the sort to treat them with respect. While he was dusting them – picking up each animal in turn and rubbing it gently and then returning it to its position – he thought about Elizabeth, and while he was thinking about Elizabeth, Diane insinuated herself into the room on tiptoe.

'It's just coming up for two o'clock, Mr Payne. Shall I go and see if the Williamses are in the waiting-room?'

He declined her offer. Her exaggerated and ingratiating steps annoyed him, and in any case she knew that unless he was exceptionally hard pressed he liked to fetch his patients from the waiting room himself. All the partners did, except for Hopwood. It was part of the psychology of confidence, and at the same time it allowed an inconspicuous visit to the staff lavatory, a door marked Private on the half landing.

Oh Elizabeth, thought Dennis as he went down the stairs, where are you now?

The following morning he woke a full hour before the alarm was due to go off at seven. It had been a hot night and was already a hot day; the sheets were damp and his pyjama jacket sodden. He lay very still, his eyes fixed on a triangle of brilliant light at the top of the window where the flowered curtains failed to meet. Elizabeth would still be asleep, he decided. A picture of her sleeping began to take shape. She lay on her back in a pale blue nightdress of satiny material, her golden hair floating out (as though she were under water) on the pillow. He could see her white neck and shoulders quite clearly, but her face refused to come into focus. To get over this difficulty, he turned her on to her side, so that her face was buried in the pillow and so that he could concentrate on her shoulder blades and the delicate and vulnerable little bumps of her backbone –

'Are you awake, dear?'

'Yes,' he said, 'I expect you'd like a cup of tea.' His hand, searching guiltily for Sheila's hand, met with a roll of rucked-up wincyette nightdress and bony hip.

Throughout the morning the temperature continued to rise. It was in the high seventies by the time he opened the waiting-room door for the last appointment.

Three-quarters of an hour later, and sweating heavily, he reached the park gates. He examined the tennis courts with unobtrusive care: they were all occupied, but there was no sign of Elizabeth. He made a hurried tour of the park benches. A golden head drew him, heart thumping, to a bench by the lily pond, but the profile belonging to the hair was not hers. The pain of this disappointment was new and almost pleasurable, and he considered it as he tagged on to a little crowd that had formed round the bandstand, where the St. John's Comprehensive School Band were making an enthusiastic hash of a selection from *My Fair Lady*, a show he and Sheila had enjoyed back in the sixties. He put a pound in the collecting tin a youth in a black and gold blazer held out to him, noticing only after he'd forced the coin through a slit too small for the job, that his money was destined not for Cancer Research or Save the Children, or even Brass Band Funds, but for Your Leisure Centre. Turning his back on the bandstand, he picked his way through sunbathers and discarded ice-cream cartons until he reached the little stream that ran the length of the park and formed its western parameter, and sat down on the bank. With his hands clasped round his knees he stared down at the trickle of water pushing its way round the lily leaves. Snatches of 'I Could Have Danced All Night', Sheila's favourite (sad, really, dancing being something she could never do) wafting from the bandstand, gave way to 'On the Street Where You Live' and then, after a couple of false starts, to 'I've Grown Accustomed to Her Face'.

'I am in love,' he said aloud. 'I am mad.' He took his coat off and then his shoes, and stretched out, eyes closed, in the sun.

'It's too early,' Sheila said again, more irritably this time. 'We could easily have another frost before June.'

It was after lunch on Saturday. Standing on the terrace in glaring sunshine, they were arguing about the pelargoniums, which had sat around the house since last October, sticky with greenfly and dropping sickly spotted leaves on all the sills. He was longing to get them out into the tubs.

'Anyway,' Sheila nodded at the tubs, where dead wallflowers leaned woody stems against each other for support, 'the wallflowers aren't over yet.'

It was too hot to argue. The Atco was back, and he mowed the lawn while Sheila rested on a recliner under a clump of silver birches at the bottom of the garden.

'Don't overdo it, love!' she called out, as for the umpteenth time he grunted past her with the grass box on his way to the compost heap.

'I was thinking of stopping for a bit – blast! I've got oil on my trousers.' He collapsed beside her on the bald sand under the birches. 'I feel a bit queasy as a matter of fact.'

Sheila put down *A Woman of Substance* and her spectacles on a little cushion of dandelions and groped for her stick under the chair.

'You sit here, and I'll go and make a cup of tea.'

He watched her mount the terrace steps. 'That is my wife,' he said aloud, as his eyes followed the bent figure in blue stretch trousers that ballooned round her thighs grotesquely, like a clown's.

He did feel queasy, and his head ached. Heart attack symptoms, he knew. Or stroke. He put a hand under his shirt and held it over his pounding heart. But there was no real pain or tightness in his chest; no pins and needles or numbness in his arms, and after a minute or two he withdrew his hand. Sheila would need help with the tray.

Halfway up the bank he thought: only two and a bit days till I see her; and he stopped and sat down again and plucked a grass stem and chewed it. Where had Elizabeth been all week? (He had searched the park every day for her in vain.) Where was she this weekend? What was she doing and with whom? He selected another stem and crunched along its length: there were three little joints in it that proved particularly satisfying. When he'd flattened it, he chose another and started again. She was sunbathing, in all likelihood, lying on her stomach with her head in her arms. In the hollows at the base of her spine tiny pearls of perspiration twinkled on minute gold hairs . . . . No – he staggered to his feet and mimed a forehand drive into the heathers – she was playing tennis on her parents' court. The Spensers lived in a Queen Anne, or was it Williams and Mary, house, half an hour away, in Hampshire. He had seen the house from the road and coveted it.

He felt worse after tea, and as the evening wore on, not queasy but sick. A band of pain, starting above his eyes, cut through his temples and burst out of the back of his head. At nine, having eaten no supper, he took a mixing bowl from the kitchen cupboard and put himself to bed in Donald's old room next to the bathroom, the bowl beside him on Donald's boy-sized chair. After an hour's uneasy dozing he was suddenly wide awake: someone was stabbing him in the stomach: someone was pulling a rope round his throat. He only just had time to grab the bowl.

When it was over, he felt no relief. Particles of vomit burned his gullet; the agony in his stomach increased. He stumbled to the bathroom and tipped the contents of the bowl down the lavatory. When the flush subsided, the water frothed evilly, its surface decorated with little splinters of tomato skin which, with eyes clouded by tears, he at first took for blood. He sat rocking on the cold edge of the bath. Bright orange fish, swimming busily on the sea-green wallpaper, spewed bubbles at him through rags of yellow seaweed.

'Are you all right in there, Dennis?' There was an anxious tapping on the door. As if to answer her, he was sick again.

150

'It's gastric flu,' Sheila informed him after he'd vomited bile at ten-minute intervals throughout the night, and after she'd consulted Doctor Benson. 'Half the town's got it.' He felt relieved and disappointed at this news, and turned on to his side, drawing his knees up in an attempt to ease the pain.

'You're to stay there for two days at least, and not get out of bed except to pay a visit. And you can't go back to work till Thursday at the earliest, preferably next week, he says. All right, pet?'

He did not mind this last injunction; he was certain he would not live till Thursday.

'I've spoken to Tom Branksome and to Diane,' Sheila's inexorable voice went on. 'They'll put off all your routine appointments, and split the urgent ones between the partners.'

'Thank you,' he murmured into the top sheet. 'Well done.'

He wished she would go. His tongue was furred and foul. His head, chest, abdomen and buttocks had been punched and kicked. Someone had drilled his joints and filled the cavities with cement. A sizeable chunk of his backbone was missing.

It was not until Monday lunch-time that, propped against the pillows and with an exiguous tray of steamed haddock sliding around on his knees, he realized his week's see-sawing anticipation had been for nothing: he would not be seeing Elizabeth tomorrow after all. The depression that followed this realization was mitigated a little by the certainty that she would not want to be seen by Branksome or Jefferies or Hopwood, and that she would merely postpone her appointment until he was well. This certainty lasted five minutes, after which time doubts began to erode it. Well, at five thirty he'd telephone Diane to see how they were all coping. And find out.

'You haven't managed much of that fish,' Sheila said in disappointed tones when she came to collect his tray. She put the tray on Donald's chest of drawers, then hobbled to the window and opened it as wide as it would go.

'That's better. It was very stuffy in here.'

He agreed that it had been. The little breeze that entered was refreshing. It ruffled the faded curtains, disturbing the orderly guardsmen in their pattern, and at the same time provoked a dusty Airfix Messerschmitt, suspended from the ceiling light on a piece of cotton thread, to fly backwards, then forwards, then back again. It lost height, came back to the centre, and then spun dizzily, its right wing dipping. He drew his legs out of her way as Sheila sat down on the bed.

'You shouldn't come near me,' he said. 'I don't want you to get this bug.' She shrugged at this and smiled. The smile creased her cheeks into a network of criss-cross puckerings, reminding him of a shrunk balloon.

'You look a little better today,' Sheila said, peering at him. She laid her hand on the bump in the bedclothes that was his knee. 'How do you feel?'

He felt, although light-headed and despite blotting paper legs, better after a bath. Back in Donald's room, he found the bed had been made up with clean sheets. Mrs D. was there, flicking a duster over his paperbacks.

'Better today, are we?' she said, as he stood helplessly in his pyjamas, waiting for her to leave.

'Shan't be two ticks – then I'll be out of your way. I don't want the flu, I can tell you.' She stuck the duster in the pocket of her straining overall and unplugged the hoover. When she'd gone, an unpleasant smell – a combination, perhaps, of sweat and Johnson's lavender wax – hung in the air like a threat.

At five-thirty on the dot, in the middle of a thunderstorm, he telephoned the surgery.

'*I* was going to phone *you*,' Diane said, after she'd enquired how he was. 'Everything's fine here, Mr Payne. Mr Branksome and Mr Jefferies have seen three of your patients – Mr Paton and Mrs Grant-Norland. Oh, and James Brooks. I was able to put the others off. Two cancelled with the flu, anyhow. It's an ill wind . . . ' she said, and giggled.

'You're very faint.' He could hardly hear her because of the

152

thunder and the crackling on the line. 'How are you fixed for tomorrow?'

'Pardon?'

He repeated the question, shouting it this time.

'Not too badly. I managed to contact all but two – Miss Barnard and Miss Spenser. I'll try them again after six. Look, we'll cope. You get well and don't worry! I'll phone you again tomorrow evening.'

But how could he not worry? Supposing Diane did not manage to contact Elizabeth? Supposing Elizabeth was seen by Hopwood? He had a sudden picture of Hopwood adjusting the angle of his torch; pressing the corners of Elizabeth's mouth down with his fat brown fingers; saying 'wider please'; running his fingers round her gums; and all this time Hopwood's face was very close to her face, his breath mingling with her breath . . . .

That night he dreamed he gave Elizabeth his Noah's Ark. She smiled her lovely smile at him and kept repeating: 'For me? Really? For me?' and he beamed back and nodded. Awake – and this was not his usual experience with dreams – it still seemed a realistic idea. Something had to happen to the Ark when he retired. He'd long ago dismissed the notion of leaving it to the practice, for without his supervision it was certain to get broken. On the other hand, if he took it home there was the problem of Donald's determination to have it for his children, and he knew what little Alec would do with it.But Elizabeth loved the Ark, she'd said so, and would treasure it. If he gave it to her – how and when was something he looked forward to working out later – it would be a link between them. A more significant, a more mysterious, a more binding link than marriage, or sex.

At eleven-thirty on Tuesday morning, the hour and the day of her appointment, still feeling woolly and wearing an ancient camel-hair dressing gown, he was seated at his desk in the sitting-room, paying bills and answering letters selected from a file marked 'Leisure Centre'. The telephone rang loudly in his ear. He let it ring twice and then put out a hand.

'Hallo, Dad,' said Donald's voice.

'Oh. Hello, Donald.' His heart, which had stopped at the first ring, started up again. 'How are you? I expect you'd like to speak to your mother.' It was tacitly understood by all three of them that Donald only ever rang to talk to Sheila.

'No, I wanted *you*,' Donald said. 'Are you feeling better? Me mam told me you've been proper poorly.' He spoke this in a convincing Liverpool accent. 'Poor old Dad.'

'That's nice of you, Donald.' He was touched. 'Yes, I do feel more myself today, thanks.' Donald chatted on for ten minutes, long distance from Southport at his practice's expense (the call made possible, he explained, because one of his patients hadn't turned up), regaling Dennis with the latest bons mots of his grandchildren. 'And guess what? Alec can actually read!'

While Donald was talking, Dennis stared out disconsolately at his newly-mown lawn, littered, after the storm, with twigs and whole branches and smashed chestnut leaves and candles. Blossoms from the laburnum and lilac bushes at the gate had been blown as far as the terrace and lay limply on the pink paving stones which steamed now in fitful sunshine. When he could get a word in, he described this desolate scene to Donald.

'Rough winds do shake the darling buds of May, you know,' said Donald sagely. 'Take care, Dad. Don't overdo it. No raking, mind.' He rang off. He hadn't even sent love to his mother, Dennis realized afterwards, with astonishment.

Uncomfortable and sweaty in his dressing-gown, he had a bath after lunch and then, dressed in proper clothes, sat in a deck-chair reading, or pretending to read, the paper. As the time for Diane's promised call approached, he became more agitated and anxious. If she hadn't telephoned by five forty-five, he'd ring her. He'd decided this at lunch-time.

The bell that rang at five thirty-eight was the front-door bell. Dennis, hovering by the telephone in the sitting-room, could hear Sheila's dot-and-carry-one progress from the kitchen, across the

Marley-tiled hallway to the front door; could hear her struggle with the catch, and then a man's voice, followed by Sheila's saying: 'Do come in, won't you. Yes, he's up. He's in the lounge, I think, or may be on the patio.'

'Don't move,' Hopwood said as Dennis, having taken the telephone off the hook before the door opened, started to push himself out of the chair he had hastily arranged himself in.

'I promised Alison I'd collect Miranda on my way home. She's at a kids' party somewhere in this neck of the woods, so I thought I'd just pop in for a moment and see how you're doing.'

'Very good of you,' Dennis said. This was the stuff that nightmares were made of. 'I'm fine. Much better.'

'You look washed-out,' Hopwood said. 'I gather it's a very nasty bug – Yes, please, if you're making one ' – he turned to Sheila who was offering a cup of tea. 'I've got to be at somewhere called Ferndale Road by six-fifteen,' he went on as Sheila left the room. 'I'm not exactly sure where it it. These little roads all look alike to me.'

'It's no distance. Have a chair. Please.'

Dennis was nettled by the 'these little roads' remark. Hopwood lived three miles out of town, up a track and in a thatched cottage, with two acres of old-world garden and a paddock that would contain Miranda's pony when she was old enough to ride one. He was always boring the partners with talk of what he called his 'place'. The Paynes had never been invited there.

'You pleased with your Escort? Noticed it in the garage. The 1.6. is quite nippy, I imagine – ' Hopwood, whose scarlet Alfa Romeo had startled the practice when he'd first turned up in it, was flushed and breathy. He had fallen too far back in the sofa cushions, and was struggling to right himself.

'All right so far. Yes, I think so. It goes.' Dennis was uninterested in motor cars. He would not have parted with his old Rover if it had not begun to let him down so badly and so often.

'I hope you're managing at the practice,' he heard himself say,

155

his hands suddenly clammy with sweat. 'Did you see any of my patients today?'

This question was not answered immediately because at that moment Sheila appeared with the trolley and Hopwood, telling Dennis to stay put, struggled out of the sofa to give her a hand and to make a space for a plate of tea-cakes on a table cluttered with knitting and knitting patterns and Sheila's prized collection of china cats. Then there was the business of pouring out the tea, and who took sugar and who wanted a tea-cake. When all this had been resolved, and Hopwood was back on the sofa – perched, this time – with a cup of tea on his knee, Sheila excused herself: 'I've got something on the cooker' – and he was alone again with Hopwood.

'You were asking me – ?' Hopwood stirred his tea. 'Oh yes. I remember. No, I didn't see any of your patients. I was a bit annoyed about that, if you must know. I had a cancellation myself and easily could have done.' He paused for a moment, perhaps expecting Dennis to make some sort of comment. 'I gather Johnny (Johnny! thought Dennis, *Jefferies* to you) had a rather unpleasant experience with one of them. He's going to phone you about it this evening.'

'What do you mean?'

'I'm a bit dodgy on the facts,' Hopwood said, so perhaps you should wait to hear them from the horse's mouth. But I understood that the woman Johnny saw had an epulis on the gum, and he's convinced it's a nasty.'

There was a silence, at the end of which Dennis managed to say: 'They're usually benign, you know.' Perhaps even now, secondaries were forming in Elizabeth's white neck. He wanted to ask Hopwood if he knew the name of the patient; but found that he couldn't.

'Maybe,' said Hopwood, 'but Johnny seemed certain. He's seen nasties before – as I imagine you must have done, in your time.' Dennis had, on at least four occasions. He was not likely to forget the shock of those discoveries; the offensive smell; the having to remain calm and matter-of-fact with the patient. And then passing the buck to some hapless G.P.: 'Look – this is not really a dental problem. You ought to see your doctor about it without delay. If you would kindly give me his name and address, I'd like to write him a little note, if I may . . .' Remaining calm and matter-of-fact was what he now had to do with Hopwood who had launched into an attack on John Jefferies for not calling him in to inspect the mouth in question. It was important, surely, that he, Hopwood, should know what to look for and to recognize, should one of his patients . . . etc.

Dennis was only half listening. His thoughts had raced back to the conversation he'd had with Elizabeth in the park. She'd said something about a sore place in her mouth. Where? Tongue. He was sure she'd said tongue. And Hopwood had mentioned an epulis, a tumour that restricted itself to the bone or gum. What's more, she was too young. Mouth tumours, whatever their nature, seldom appeared before middle age. And she wasn't a smoker, he was certain. She couldn't be. No, the patient had to be Miss Barnard, the English mistress at St Theresa's with whom he sometimes had convivial chat about the Metaphysical Poets. She was about the right age, and she smoked like a chimney. He felt enormously relieved by his deductions, and offered Hopwood a third cup of tea.

Hopwood, declining, got to his feet and put his cup on the trolley.

'Johnny did say there was something unusual – peculiar – about this case, but I'm blowed if I can remember what it was.'

Bastard, Dennis thought. Bastard. He felt, suddenly, very tired and very old. How could life, how could Hopwood, how could *Elizabeth*, do this to him? What had he done to deserve it? Without knowing it, they'd managed to kill off his innocent pastime. He would never now give her the Ark. For he saw at once that even if it wasn't Elizabeth, even if there was nothing seriously wrong with her mouth at all – a minor infection, a touch of uloglossitis, could easily account for the symptoms she'd described

157

– he would always associate her with this appalling afternoon, and Hopwood's red face against the sofa cushions.

Grist

'All my love for you, Sweet*heart*,' he always said. He invariably said. 'All my love for *you*.' So when one night he didn't say it, Babe knew he didn't love her. She waited until next time – the next time his body relaxed on hers – to be sure. But it was only a formality. For by then, the space of two or three days, there were other signs. He stopped touching, fingering, you might say, with one long finger, her shoulder blades and her arms, in the way he did (as though he were drawing pictures on them). He stopped shovelling dog shit from the lawn. He didn't bring surprise whiskies to the ironing board. In their supermarket, he no longer vanished in Cereals so that he could materialize seconds later in the Pet Food aisle: 'Excuse me. You are the Most Beautiful Person in the World, and I claim my Lifetime of Happiness.' A talkative man at home, a mimic, a raconteur, he became silent. His silence grew and grew and filled the house. It was October, and the grass hidden by a weight of wet chestnut leaves, but he, usually the first to attack onerous tasks and the last to abandon them, seemed not to notice. When Babe got out the rake and barrow and started to pull the leaves into heaps, he put on his old garden coat, the garment of his she liked the best, and went for a walk by himself. (He, who'd never allowed her to take so much as a step without him!)

A horrible ten days passed, in which he pretended black was white and white black, in which he played the torturing husband in *Gaslight*, while Babe was stuck with the Ingrid Bergman role (but without Bergman's beauty; without the sure and certain hope

161

of rescue before the credits). At the end of the ten days they had a show down. He turned everything they'd shared on its head. Then he cleared out his darkroom, packed his belongings and left.

When Babe felt able to, she drove over to Aunt's and told her about it. Not all of it, and not all at once. Babe was seeing a lot of Aunt just then. Aunt was dying, or, more accurately, living with Death. Death was giving Aunt a hard time. He followed her up and down stairs, and from sitting-room to kitchen; he had a sweetish, stomach-turning smell. He leant over her shoulder when she was playing patience or doing *The Times* crossword, he kept her awake all night. Aunt had no time for Death, and she didn't want to give him cottage room. Apart from her animals, she'd always lived alone. Depending on the strength of her pain, and on the weather, she fought or ignored him. Or she mocked him. Once, when she'd chucked Babe a cigarette and lit one for herself, she offered the packet over her shoulder. 'Go on,' she said, shaking the pack impatiently, 'take one. Feel free. It'll do you good. He's a humourless bugger,' she said to Babe.

Aunt smoked like a chimney, and the ceiling above the corner table where she did the crossword and played round after round of patience was dark brown, like the ceiling in a pub. Those who loved Aunt found this strange, it seemed out of keeping, because in all other respects Aunt was fastidious. Even with three cats and a dog, there was nothing messy about her tiny sitting room. Except for the overflowing ashtray, of course. Still, as Aunt said, you couldn't worry about getting cancer when you already had it.

Babe convinced herself that telling Aunt her troubles might, if not cheer Aunt up exactly, at least give her something else to think about (although Aunt was always interested in other people; always thinking about them). Aunt was upset by Babe's news. Upset for Babe and upset, in a way, for herself. And surprised. She hadn't seen it coming. Only the month before, Babe had brought his new book of photographs, just published, for her to see. 'That *is* nice,' Aunt had said, looking at the flyleaf on which he'd written 'Your Book, from Your Person' and underneath, his initial, enclosed by a heart. (Babe hadn't told Aunt then her worries about private, lovey-dovey inscriptions, the awful poignancy of them in secondhand bookshops: 'Binkie, Beloved Angel – All My Love for Always, Tiddles. Xmas, 1926.' 'For Clive – as fine a man as any girl could wish for – Denise.' But she had told *him*. And he'd smiled. And drawn a picture on her shoulder blades.) Aunt had sat at her table with the book of photographs, turning the pages slowly, studying each one. There were shots of Babe's grown up sons; views of her house and garden the photographer had called home. There was a whole section devoted to portraits of Babe. 'Is that really you?' Aunt had asked, peering. 'It's not the you I know. I'm not sure I want to see you in bed. Do I?' Aunt had said, of another, 'Though I must say your chins are tactfully lit.'

Aunt was upset by Babe's news. She'd grown fond of the photographer, as she always referred to him. He was interesting; he brought another world into her sitting room; he made her laugh. She was sorry she wouldn't be seeing him anymore. Having admitted that, having got it off her chest ('Look, I've got it off my chest,' she said, cough-laughing into her whisky glass) Aunt did everything she could to make Babe feel better and more positive.

'A nice fellow. Clever, certainly – though not at crosswords. Or was he?' Aunt said, 'A joke, ho ho. Generous? Oh yes. You're still hung about with his baubles, I see. Handsome, I won't deny. But a juvenile lead. Not man enough for you. Not mature enough. No. Let's have another whisky.'

They drank pints of whisky, interspersed, in Aunt's case, with painkillers and minute helpings of the creamed vegetable soup – usually carrot – those who loved Aunt took it in turns to make and bring her. Her fridge, and the box freezer above it, were full of the stuff, in little cling-filmed pots, jostling with the cod fillets Aunt fed to her cats. Every so often Aunt would leave the room, and patter, rice-paper thin, to the kitchen; and return with a fizzing glass of what looked like fruit salts which she'd set down beside her whisky on the table. Morphine every four hours; solpadine (the fizzers) as a supplementary when the pain got unbearable; and all

163

that whisky – why didn't it kill her?

'What did it mean, Aunt? Was none of it true? Was it a game?' Babe asked her. (Babe was still in shock; it had been so sudden.) 'Was it only a game?'

'Could be,' Aunt said. 'How do I know? Yes I do. I'm sure he meant it. I'm sure he thought he meant it, at the time. Anyway, don't you play games? You always beat me at Scrabble, I notice. I think you cheat. Don't expect me to play with you in future. Now, getting back to the crossword,' Aunt said, 'Harpo and Groucho won't do – sorry chaps, no offence – so who were the others? Tell.'

'Chico?' Babe said. She was no good at the crossword (which Aunt regularly solved in ten minutes) but it was nice to be consulted. Aunt always consulted her. 'Then there was Karl, of course,' Babe said.

'*Karl*,' Aunt said, 'Karl. How could we forget him? Quite the funniest of the four.'

A day or so later, a postcard came to Babe's house, written all over in Aunt's famous blue felt tip: 'What say HARPO, GROUCHO, CHICO& ??? ZEPPO ??? So we don't need ~~Lenin~~ Karl (!) Come back SOON. XXX Aunt.'

Aunt's ceiling seemed to grow browner as they sat there, evening after evening, puffing away, swigging away, drunk as life peeresses. Soon snow pressed against the windows. Soon the lanes were full of it. Sometimes Babe had to stay the night, and she lay in the double bed in Aunt's spare room and listened to her cough, and heard her pad to the bathroom time and time again. The light under Aunt's door stayed on until morning.

'We laughed a lot,' Babe told Aunt. 'We were always laughing. Doubled up with it, often. Our cheekbones ached. We did have fun you know. We had a lot of fun.'

'I know you did,' Aunt said, 'I know you did. Laughter's good stuff. I approve of laughter. Tastes better than these fizzers, yuk,' Aunt said. 'A good howl can be therapeutic, too.'

Aunt didn't howl, so far as Babe knew, but she wasn't always able to laugh. Sometimes when Babe telephoned she was sharp. No, she wasn't all right, she was bloody awful. No, Babe couldn't come over. No, no, no. Not today and not tomorrow. Not any day this week.

Christmas cards began to appear on Aunt's chimneypiece. They didn't talk about them. Aunt was dreading Christmas. Not because she'd acknowledged it would be her last (she was making plans for her garden in the Spring: 'Shall I build that wall?' she kept asking, 'What do you think? Give me your views. Should I move the island bed? Should I widen the border?') but because she'd always hated festivals. Festivals were for children. Aunt had had affairs, successful and less successful, happy and not so happy; Aunt loved men and liked them, but she'd never married and she'd never had children. In the past, those who loved Aunt had begged her to spend Christmasses with them and their children (of whom she was varyingly fond) and sometimes she had, providing it didn't mean spending a night away from home. Aunt's old maroon Mini hadn't left its garage now for two weeks. She wouldn't be going anywhere of her own choosing. Her loved ones would be popping in, of course, on Christmas Eve and Christmas Day and Boxing Day; they'd all be bringing presents and booze and fags and carrot soup; Mr Timms from across the road would be coming midday to make up her fire; the doctor and the nurse would call. But there was no getting away from it: some of the time, a great deal of the time, and all of every night, Aunt was going to be – apart from the animals – alone over the Christmas holiday. With him.

Aunt still hadn't accepted her lodger. She was still taking swipes at him, still keeping him at a short arm's length. How, nobody knew. There was nothing of her. The nurse was 'dropping in' every day now, sometimes twice. The morphine was three-hourly. 'One of the advantages of teabags,' Aunt said, peering into the tea she invariably let go cold before drinking – or, increasingly, not drinking – 'is there's no risk of a tall dark stranger lurking in the cup. So there,' she said over her shoulder to him. 'Yah boo to you know who,' she said to Babe.

While Aunt was out of the room getting her fizzers, Babe peeked inside the Christmas cards on Aunt's chimneypiece. She'd thought there might be one from the photographer. He hadn't sent one to Babe, and she was trying not to think of last year, and the fun they'd had, the fun she'd thought they'd had – but Aunt, why no card for Aunt? He hadn't fallen out of love with *her*. Yet he had been fond of her, he'd said so, often. 'Aunt is a major human being,' he'd said, more than once, 'really major,' and Babe had agreed, even though, in her view, major was a word best left to military matters. No card for Aunt, no card for a really major human being, hurt. At a hurtful time, it was one of the things that hurt most. The photographer had had to write to Babe once or twice – brief, typewritten notes on practical subjects, things he'd left behind and so forth, and stamped with a second class stamp – but he'd never mentioned Aunt in these notes, he'd never asked how she was, he'd never sent her his love. Babe kept turning this over in her mind. She stayed awake pondering this. Was nothing good? Was nothing true? Was nothing real? Did nothing mean anything?

Babe couldn't talk to Aunt about this, of course, but there were other things that hurt, and she told Aunt about those.

'This exhibition is painful,' Babe said. 'All those portraits of me. More or less naked. Asleep. In bed. I'm even on the catalogue. And last week in the colour supplement there was one of *her* – his new person. Naked. In bed. We'll be beside each other, you realize, on the ICA walls. Bedfellows, so to speak. How can he do that, Aunt? Why doesn't it bother him? How can he do it so soon?'

'All grist to the photographer's mill,' Aunt said, trying to get a spoonful of carrot soup into her mouth; failing; giving up. 'Anything goes with artists. All must be sacrificed to Art – is photography Art? I'm never quite sure – nothing, no one, is safe. Anyway, they aren't portraits of you or of her, they're portraits of him. He's the subject of all his photographs, even those fuzzy landscapes. That's enough profundities for the time being. I'm not sure I like carrot soup all that much,' Aunt said, 'if I ever did. Could you pass the word round?'

'Do you think he's claimed a Lifetime of Happiness from her yet?' Babe asked Aunt over the telephone. Babe had rung Aunt to tell her Boris had come home. He'd been missing two days, unusual for him, and she'd been frantic. Aunt had been anxious about Boris too, and had rung before breakfast for news – which meant a painful descent of the stairs because she had no telephone by her bed. Those who loved Aunt were working on her to get one connected.

'I once knew a cat who was away eight months, and then just walked in,' Aunt had said before breakfast. 'What a relief,' she'd said a moment ago, when Babe had told her the glad tidings. 'Now we can all relax. Until next time.'

'Do you suppose he's sold her one?' Babe persisted. (She referred to the occasion the photographer had pretended to be a salesman, and had come to her door offering a Lifetime of Happiness on an easy instalment plan.)

'What's a lifetime?' Aunt said. She'd just 'celebrated', the one she loved best had helped her 'celebrate', her sixty-third birthday. 'What's happiness? Anyway, did *you* buy it? Did you say Ta ever so, and sign on the dotted line? I doubt it,' Aunt said. 'Not you. Too dull. Too commonplace. You'd never commit yourself to that.'

'Look, Babe,' Aunt said later, as they sat either side her fire, 'you must try and get a sense of proportion about all this. If Jim and Ted,' she said, referring to Babe's sometime husbands, 'merit a section, say, in Ted's case, and a chapter in Jim's, then the photographer is worth only a page or so in your book. I'm speaking figuratively of course. Only a page or so. Half a dozen, at the most. Remember that.' Aunt, after two stabs at it, swallowed her morphine mix, and a made a face; and then chased the morphine with a swig of whisky. Just recently she'd given up all attempts at soup, no matter what variety, though she toyed with a forkful of scrambled egg, a spoonful of jelly.

167

'Incidentally,' Aunt said, 'how's your other book coming along? My book, I should say.' (For Babe had asked permission to dedicate the book she was writing – not writing; how could she? – to Aunt. Aunt had said yes. She was flattered, she said, not to say bowled over – though she did rather hope there wouldn't be any filth in it. No explicit bedroom scenes. Nothing a maiden aunt wouldn't be pleased to read. Babe wanted to finish the book in time for Aunt, but she knew she hadn't a hope.) 'Does the photographer appear in your book in some guise or other?' Aunt said. 'Do I? Are we both a bit of grist to your mill?'

After Aunt died, Babe said to the one Aunt loved best, the one who loved Aunt best, the one who had lost most: 'What shall we do without Aunt? What shall we do without Aunt's voice, and Aunt's laugh, and Aunt's famous blue felt tip and Aunt's postcards? How shall we manage without Aunt to tell things to?'

The one Aunt loved best and who loved Aunt best and who had lost most, the one to whom Aunt wrote not just postcards, but long letters (and had managed to do so from her hospice bed that last harrowing week) said: 'We must go on talking to Aunt. We must keep telling her things. Aunt was always interested. You can tell her about the awful men you meet, and the boring dinner parties you go to. You can tell her when Boris goes missing, and when he comes back. If you feel like cutting your throat, tell Aunt.

Tell Aunt everything. Make Aunt laugh.'

Babe told Aunt. She told her funny things and sad things and boring things; and afterwards she imagined what Aunt's response would be.

For a time it worked. For a time, Babe could hear Aunt's laugh, and Aunt's cough and Aunt's voice. For a time, she could see Aunt. She could see her lighting a cigarette, and padding about with a glass in her hand. She could see Aunt's hand in close-up, turning up the cards, flattening out the crossword page on the table in the corner.

Babe devised all manner of ruses to keep Aunt there, and for a time it worked, but it got harder. It got harder every day. She forgot to tell Aunt, or she couldn't face it, or she put it off. Then when she did, she couldn't always hear Aunt's reply. After two months had gone by, she couldn't see Aunt's face or Aunt's hands in the way she had; she couldn't hear Aunt's voice distinctly, she couldn't see Aunt clearly at all.

Then one day Babe went out to dinner, and when she got home, around midnight, and was having a nightcap, she told Aunt about her evening.

'Aunt,' Babe said, sitting in her easy chair, sipping her whisky, 'here's one for you. I've just been to a dinner party. Not good news, as per. No ashtrays for a start. When I asked for one, my hostess, laughing a v. false laugh, said: "You're not still a slave to that disgusting habit, surely? I thought no one in their right minds was silly enough to smoke these days," etc, etc. Then, would you believe, Bobby Gaskell – who knows the answer perfectly well – asked me why the photographer wasn't there. Had I left him at home, or something? "I got the impression he never left your side," he said. Great. Then we went in to dinner. The first course was soup. "Carrot soup!" the woman opposite me exclaimed. "My favourite! How clever of you, Annabel! Such a fiddle faddle to make, but worth it. One can never have too much carrot soup!" '

The story was supposed to make Aunt laugh, it was supposed to make Babe laugh, they were supposed to laugh together. But perhaps Babe had drunk too much claret before her nightcap; perhaps she hadn't told the story right; because though she waited in the quiet room in the quiet house, she couldn't hear anything. Babe went on sitting there, drawing on her cigarette, draining her whisky glass, listening; and eventually she thought she could hear Aunt, a long way off, saying ho ho *ho*. She thought she could hear Aunt laugh. Babe wanted to join in. She wanted to laugh with Aunt; for a moment she thought she was going to, but she didn't. She howled. She howled up the stairs and into the bathroom and while she was getting undressed and while she was taking her face off. She cried herself to sleep.

Noble Rot

It was on her way back from the hairdresser that Cecily Bressingham saw the picnickers in the lay-by. The lay-by was on the left of the main road, a hundred yards from the crossroads where, in order to get home, Cecily Bressingham turned right. As she waited, indicator ticking, for the traffic to go by, she thought how extraordinary the lower orders were. Who in their right minds, in the middle of the most lovely countryside, and on this boiling hot day, would choose to picnic in a *lay-by,* only inches from this horrendous main road? It was not just extraordinary, it was – she remembered the white head of one, the bald head of the other – pathetic. And pathetically sad. How wonderful it would be to rescue them and transport them to her own garden; to the shade of a willow tree and the peace of the river bank . . . .

Cecily, who since childhood had maintained a partiality for fairy-tale endings, was subject to fantasies of this sort – the sort that allowed her a starring, dragon-slaying role; but commonsense and a busy life usually prevented their being translated into realities. So she sighed, and when there was a gap in the lorries, turned right on to the B road, and then left in to the lane that wound, with passing places only, to the valley where she lived.

Halfway down the lane she stopped; and reversed the car into a field, and drove back the way she'd come.

Arnold had laid the table with the knives and forks Elaine had given them for their silver wedding, and was unscrewing the thermos, when a big grey car pulled on to the lay-by and parked behind his car.

'Blow,' Gladys said, shading her spectacles and squinting, 'Don't look now, but we've got company.'

A woman in jeans and a tee-shirt got out of the car and came over to them.

'Good morning,' the woman said.

'Afternoon,' Arnold said, not looking up. He poured tea into a cup and handed it to Gladys. Gladys put her cup on the table and squinted suspiciously at the stranger, who said – but whatever she said was lost as a juggernaut thundered up the hill. The ground shook, the table jumped; and in the lorry's wake, the black grasses at the roadside rolled inland like waves to a shore. The stranger squatted beside Gladys's chair and rested her hand on the table top.

'Look, forgive me for interfering,' she said, 'but I passed you a moment ago, and I'm very worried about you both. I know this road well,' she continued, speaking the words slowly and clearly. 'It is very, very dangerous, and you are much too near it. Where have you come from?' she asked, looking from one to the other with an expression of interest and concern, 'Where are you going to?'

'Swindon way,'Arnold said, in answer to the first question – though what business it was of hers he couldn't see. 'We're all right, thanks. No need to worry about us,' he said. 'This is a lay-by, for cars to lay-by in. That's what it's for.'

Gladys picked up her cup and took a sip from it. Perhaps their visitor was a plain-clothes policewoman, or a social worker. 'We was sat in this field a while back,' she said pleasantly, 'but then this tractor come up and asks us to move.' As she spoke, a petrol tanker, pursued by a container lorry, pursued in turn by an estate car, chuntered past, and sprayed them with an oily exhaust.

'Look,' the woman shouted, when they'd finished coughing, 'I live just over there, beyond that hill, and I'd love it, I'd be really delighted, if you'd come and eat your picnic in our garden –'

'We couldn't do that.' Arnold was firm. They could've eaten their picnic in their own garden, if they'd wanted.

'– by the river, under the weeping willows' – the woman turned to Gladys – 'in the shade . . .'

A river. Shade. Peace. Quiet. Gladys patted her perm and considered these attractions. She had always liked a river, in fact only the other day –

'You don't know us, and we don't know you,' Arnold said, determined to end the discussion.

'My name is Cecily Bressingham,' the woman said to Gladys, 'How do you do?'

'I'm Gladys Carter,' Gladys said, 'and this is my husband, Arnold.' Arnold nodded, but said nothing. Instead, he took a handkerchief from his trouser pocket and blotted his neck and forehead. The heat was terrible. A man who'd served with the Eighth Army was hardly one to be afraid of an English summer, as he was fond of saying, but – as he was also fond of saying – he was not as young as he used to be; and he winced now as two motor bikes, competing for the summit, raced up the hill.

Cecily Bressingham saw the wince, and decided to play her trump card. This was an Accident Black Spot, she told them, with at least one fatal smash a month. There were plans to widen the road, or to make it a dual carriageway, but until then –

'Oh Arnold,' Gladys said.

Arnold gave in.

'Well, this is an adventure!' Gladys said later as they waited behind the grey car at the crossroads.

'I don't like it,' Arnold said. 'I don't like being pushed round. What d'you think she's playing at?'

She wasn't playing at anything, Gladys told him, she wasn't going to turn them into toadstools, she was just being kind. There wasn't enough kindness in the world these days. It had been dangerous in that lay-by, she reproved him, and smelly, and hot. They should've taken that turning left by the garage where she'd said.

In the lane the grey car braked in a passing place to let a tractor and silage cart go by, and Arnold's car nearly ran into the back of it.

'You two all right?' Cecily Bressingham called cheerfully out of her window. 'Sorry about that! Nearly there now.'

The road meandered downhill between low hedges, over which they could see sheep on one side and young corn on the other. In front of them the downs rolled away, pale grey-green fading to grey-blue, here and there a snippet of yellow, almost treeless.

'In the old days, that would've been mustard,' Arnold lamented.

'Imagine this place in winter, Arn,' Gladys said. 'Think of it in snow.' But when she tried to herself, she couldn't. It was too hot.

At the bottom of the hill they passed a farm with a cluster of barns and a grain silo and cattle standing in a caked yard, and after that a group of cottages with pink roses and purple clematis growing over them. A couple of bends, and then into view came the double row of poplars that, no matter how often she saw them, always reminded Cecily of the Loire valley, their leaves glittering – like tinsel, Gladys decided – in the sunshine.

'Look Arnold – the river!' she said, but it was no more than a stream at this point, and Arnold told her so. He had not yet recovered his humour, and the car, despite all the windows being down, was an oven. 'Some five minutes,' he said, referring to the amount of time Mrs Whateverhernamewas had said it took to get there.'

They passed a pub called 'The Dove' on the left of the road, and a village shop with a PO sign and an ice cream banner on the right. They passed more cottages, grey stone and thatched, and a village hall with an asbestos roof.

'Must be that place, I bet,' Gladys said, as the car in front slowed to a crawl, and the high stone wall appeared on the right. Behind it they could see a square house, painted white, with black window frames. But no. The grey car slid past it and on round a bend between high banks. When they caught up with it again, its left indicator was blinking.

Beyond a stretch of park railing they followed the car sharp left over a cattle grid, through stone pillars surmounted by a fancy ironwork of ribbons and scrolls. The drive was long and full of potholes, and Arnold had to juggle with the steering wheel in order to avoid them.

'I won't have any tyres left,' he grumbled.

How do they manage when they're in a rush to catch a train? Gladys wondered.

On either side, the unfenced route was lined with cows, standing quite still, staring, and one of these lifted its tail as they passed and unconcernedly messed its rump and the ground with black-looking dung.

'It's like being in a safari park,' Gladys said. 'A bit unnerving.' What would be unnerving, Arnold thought, as the drive forked at a clump of trees and the convoy swung right on to a gravel sweep, would be to own a herd as big as this one, dairy products being considered poison these days, and the government subsidy cut by half.

After the splendour of the gates and the length of the drive, Gladys was a little disappointed at the size of the house. It was definitely large. Definitely. But not that large. Not like some of the places they'd visited. Not like Longleat, or Castle Howard, or Knole.

'You didn't tell us you was taking us to a stately home,' Arnold said, struggling with his car door as their abductress approached.

'Well, hardly that!' Cecily Bressingham tugged at Arnold's door (which eventually gave so that he fell, rather than stepped, into the drive) and laughed a merry, embarrased laugh. 'It's just an ordinary, well, manor house, I suppose you'd call it.' As she spoke, she made a squeezing gesture with her finger and thumb that reduced the edifice behind them to tied cottage proportions. 'The front's misleading, it's actually quite small, in fact.'

The Carters stood in the drive and stared up at the quite small manor house shimmering, dream-like, in the heat. They saw, or rather Arnold saw – for Gladys was short-sighted and not much interested in architectural detail – a stone porch with three Doric columns on either side of double front doors; three bay windows capped with pediments; the date 1585 on a central panel above the door. The roof was gabled along its length, and surmounting each gable was a small heraldic beast – lions they might have been, though it was hard to tell when they were so badly chipped. The house reminded Arnold of another house, but what and where he couldn't place. Feeling that some comment was called for, he remarked on the magnificent *magnolia grandiflora* that grew on the left of the porch to the height of the gables. He'd never seen one that size before, he said.

'No? Well, as a matter of fact that's a sore point, it's on its last legs. It *ought* to come down. And we *ought* to plant another, but I can't bring myself to quite yet . . . . Now, before I take you to the river – ' Cecily Bressingham turned to Gladys ' – would either of you like – ' she searched round for the right word, the word that would make them feel at home ' – the toilet? Or a wash?'

Gladys said No thank you, though she meant Yes please. It was a good hour and a half since they'd paid a visit to the convenience in Malmesbury. Her bladder was always playing her up. She didn't need to go yet awhile, but –

'Your picnic must be melting,' Cecily said, 'Let me give you a hand.' While Arnold was fighting with the boot, a man, balding, moustached, in shirt sleeves and corduroy trousers, and followed by two labrador dogs, came round the side of the house calling 'Thistle, Thistle –

'Oh there you are,' he said. 'What's happening about lunch?'

'This is my husband William,' Cecily Bressingham said. 'Mr and Mrs Carter – er, Gladys, is that right? and Albert.'

'Arnold,' Arnold said.

'We met on the main road. They couldn't find anywhere safe and nice for their picnic, and I thought the river garden would be just the place –'

'Quite right, very good, very good,' William said. 'Down, Tess.'

'We're fond of dogs,' Gladys said, and she bent down and

178

patted the black head of the one that was slobbering over her new sandals, 'aren't we Arnold?' The Bressinghams helped the Carters get their picnic things out of the car, and when everyone had something to carry – a rug, a chair, a table, an orange picnic bag – and was about to move off, a girl, wearing long black flowing garments, drifted towards them over the gravel.

'Lunch,' the girl said. 'Have you seen the boys?'

'This is Mr and Mrs Carter,' Cecily began again, with explanations. 'My daughter Olivia.'

'Oh right', Olivia said, and drifted back to the house.

'I hope your meal won't spoil,' Gladys said, as she and Arnold, fainting with heat and hunger, followed the Bressinghams and the waving tails of the labrador dogs down a stone path edged with lavender that was not yet in flower.

'Not to worry!' Cecily called over her shoulder. 'We always have bread and cheese on Saturdays!'

It really was a delightful garden. On the left a cedar-shaded lawn, planted out with croquet hoops, stretched away to a drystone wall; the giant yew hedge on the right had windows cut into it, and through these squares of brilliant light could be seen pale, flat-petalled roses and sections of herbaceous border. At the end of the path, a lead shepherdess with a dead-looking lamb under her arm gestured her crook towards a pergola, and they bent their heads to avoid ribbons of – Cecily Bressingham informed the Carters with a laugh – Paul's Himalayan Musk. Through this, and the scent of a thousand hot herbs at once rose to them from star-shaped beds, divided and edged with box.

'This is the herb garden,'Cecily said, stopping, bending down to pick a piece of something which she rubbed between her fingers and then held to her nose. 'Far too far from the kitchen, need I say.'

'Where've you come from?' William asked Arnold. They had left the herb garden and were descending a grassy slope where grew gunnera plants, the size of small trees. The ground was soft here, and the heels of Gladys's sandals sank into it, nearly toppling her several times. 'Ah,' William said, when Arnold had told him, 'the train-spotter's mecca.'

At the waterside, by drifts of mimulus and astilbes, under a weeping willow, in Paradise, the Bressinghams put up the Carters' table and chairs and laid out their rug.

'Please make yourselves at home,' Cecily said, straightening the tablecloth. (It was quite hideous, oh dear, dark brown with beige roses all over it.) 'Have a ziz after your picnic. Walk anywhere you like – the lily pond's over there; which might amuse you. We'd be very pleased if you'd join us for tea, at tea time.' Arnold said thank you, but they had to get back to feed the cats – something Gladys never did till eight or nine.

'Well if you can stay, we'd be absolutely thrilled, more than delighted. We'll send one of the children to fetch you up about four.'

'Oh lor, I forgot to offer them anything to drink,' Cecily said at lunch, which they were eating in the garden room, with the french windows wide open.

'They had a thermos, I seem to remember,' William said, stretching a sandy-haired and freckled forearm for the celery.

'No no no, I meant a proper drink. Something cold.'

'Beurre, s'il vous plait,' Mungo said, stabbing Jean-Marie with an elbow.

Frogs were the pits. Jean-Marie never passed anybody anything. Cecily turned to her daughter Sophie. Would she be a darling, and take the poor Carters a bottle of plonk and a couple of cans of beer?

'You have to be joking,' Sophie said. 'I haven't met them, I don't know them.'

'Mungo then? It's about time – '

'Can't. Sorry. Got to to go now.' Mungo looked at his watch. But it was only one twenty, and he was not due on the cricket field until two.

'Who are the Carters?' George wanted to know.

'Your mother's new best friends,' William said, 'I don't like

180

your tone.'

'They're very nice people,' Cecily said.

'Yes they're very nice people,' William said. 'By the way,' he said to his wife, 'your other best friends, the Kiftsgates, can't come tonight. Poll rang when you were out. Harry's malingering. And the Hascombes are bringing an American they've been landed with for the weekend.'

Cecily could have cried. She'd been trying for months to get the Kiftsgates and the Hascombes and the Waddesdons together for dinner, so that they could be nice to the Muckrosses who were new, and until that moment believed she had succeeded. Mungo looked at his watch again, and got up.

'I'm off now,' he said, 'if that's okay with you.'

'No,' William said. (Mungo was being a little pest these holidays, a real little pain.) 'Not until you've taken the Whatsisnames a drink, as your mother asked you.'

'I don't mind going, 'Jamie said, realizing that, lunch being nearly over, washing-up loomed.

'No, Mungo will go.'

'What bottle?' Mungo asked at the door. 'Babycham? Cherry B? A Pony? What's their poison, d'you reckon?'

He could take a Sauvignon, his father told him, and there was some lager in the fridge. 'Bottle opener, glasses, ice. Get on with it. Scram.'

The Carters were finishing off their Danish pastries, when a youth in cricket clothes and with a basket over his arm loped across the lawn, skidded down the bank and landed on the rug at their feet. They were eating their picnic bolt upright on chairs, as was their habit, and this somehow added to their air of surprise on seeing the intruder.

'Liquid refreshment, with my mother's compliments,' said Mungo, against all the odds deciding to play the charmer. 'I'm your barman.' He tipped the contents of his basket on to the rug and held up a corkscrew.

The Carters stared at him, too astonished to speak.

'It's very kind of you, dear,' Gladys said at last, 'but we've just had tea. We never touch a drop in the day time,' she added – an understatement, for, weddings and funerals apart, she and Arnold – not that they had anything against it, mind – were teetotal.

'Go on, it's a picnic. Be a devil.' Mungo hadn't run all this way in the heat to be turned down, no way.

'I'll try a beer, if that's what you've got there,' Arnold said, peering.

'Hooray! I've got a customer!' Mungo threw a can into the air and caught it – just – with one hand. 'Catch,' he said to Arnold. Arnold caught.

'Remember you're driving, Arnold,' Gladys said.

'Change your mind. Go on,' Mungo said, beaming the smile that never failed to win all female hearts, and the hearts of certain senior boys at school.

'Well, 'Gladys was wavering. It was after all, a very warm day.

'Perhaps.'

'Don't worry, this Sauvignon's quite drinkable.' Mungo held the bottle, which seemed to be not the right shape, away from him to read the label, and when he had done so, turned rather pink. Oh well, he consoled himself, nothing but the best for Mum's new best friends. And serve his father right for not fetching the bottle himself.

'You going to have one?' Arnold said, tapping his can of lager. 'Daren't.' Mungo knelt up on the rug, and indicated his cricket clothes. Then he opened the bottle and poured a glass of yellow wine and handed it to Gladys.

'School match, would it be?' Arnold asked.

'Village', Mungo said. 'We broke up last week,' he explained. Arnold was surprised. His grandsons had another three weeks of summer term left to go before the holidays.

'This wine is very pleasant,' Gladys said, sipping. 'Cheers.' It was sweet, and she liked a sweet wine, but if she was honest she'd have to say it was a shade too sweet – and heavy – to be really refreshing on such a warm day.

'What's your name, dear?' she asked, straining out of her chair to put the glass on the table.

'Mungo,' Mungo said.

'How old are you, Mango?'

'Mungo,' Mungo said. 'Fourteen.'

The Carters were very surprised. He looked much older than fourteen, they told him. 'And so tall,' Gladys said, 'and slim.' She looked reprovingly at Arnold who'd got fatter since he stopped work, and who was only five feet six.

'Mungo Park,' Arnold muttered to himself. 'Batsman or bowler?' he asked Mungo.

'Batsman,' said Mungo, whose highest score this season had been ten, whose average, three.

'Our youngest boy, Malcolm, used to play cricket,' Gladys remarked.

'Oh, right?' Mungo said, and he turned to Gladys, but she was silent, having no more to say on the subject.

'Play at school, do you?' Arnold asked. 'In the team?'

Mungo nodded. He did play in a team of sorts.

'Where's that then? Where's your school?'

'Er, Berkshire,' Mungo said, seeing embarrasment somewhere ahead, hoping to avoid it.

'Berkshire's a big place,' Arnold said. 'The Royal County of Berkshire is quite a big place.' He tipped back his head and drained the beer can.

'Slough, then,' Mungo said.

'Slough's Bucks,' Arnold said ruminitavely. 'I know' – he leant forward in his chair and pointed a finger at Mungo – 'you's at Eton College, right?'

'Right,' Mungo said, accused; found guilty.

'Like it there, do you?' Arnold was interested. He'd seen a documentary about Eton boys only recently on the TV.

Mungo considered. He thought of his housemaster whom he

disliked. Of his classical tutor who (he was pretty sure) disliked him. He wasn't good at work. He wasn't good enough at games. Most of the boys in his block were trogs or wankers. The truth was, he'd never liked school, this or any other.

'It's okay,' he said. 'What do you do?' he asked Arnold. 'What's your job?'

'Arnold's retired,' Gladys said. 'He'll be sixty-eight, come September.'

Her tone suggested that sixty-eight was a remarkable age, and one attained by very few; that she was responsible for his having achieved it, and that congratulations would not be out of order.

'I was in waste disposal,' Arnold said. 'My eldest lad runs the business now.'

Waste disposal? Waste disposal? Mungo racked his grey matter. 'Nuclear waste?'

'Sewage,' Arnold said. 'Septic tanks. Evacuation of.'

'Ah we've got one of those,' Mungo said enthusiastically. Putrefaction was one of his favourite words.

'You would have,' Arnold told him, 'out here. There'd be no mains drainage out here. What time's your cricket?'

'Oh lor, I'll be late.' Mungo leapt from the rug.

Arnold wished him luck. Gladys wished him all the best. At the last minute, Mungo remembered his manners and topped up Gladys's glass. While they'd been talking it had become a bathing pool for a wide variety of insect life, and he removed this with a finger and then propped the bottle in the roots of the weeping willow.

'I'll be pickled, you know,' Gladys said untruthfully, not wishing to offend. She could always tip the wine away afterwards.

'Goodbye,' Mungo said. He was quite sorry to swap the Carters for the cricket field, where he felt certain he was going to score a duck. He'd quite liked Arnold. Arnold was okay.

Nice enough lad, Arnold thought when Mungo had gone.

'Nice enough lad,' he said to Gladys.

'Nice manners,' Gladys agreed, 'and lovely hair – wasted on a

184

boy.' But fancy saddling him with a name like that, she thought, a name that sounded like a Latin American dance step, or one of those fruits (she and Arnold hadn't tried, and weren't likely to, at 70p a go) on the Exotic fruits counter at their supermarket.

'I'm going to have a bit of shut-eye now,' she told Arnold; and she removed her spectacles and settled more comfortably into her chair.

Arnold wasn't ready for a rest. Solidly and squarely built, he was too heavy for these flimsy picnic chairs; the metal frame of his cut painfully into the underside of his thighs, and into his back. He got up and stretched and walked about, pushing at the fronds of willow that everywhere assailed him, sniffing the river smell. On his way past Gladys's chair, the toe of his shoe caught the wine bottle lodged in the roots of the tree. It fell over at once, and the wine pumped out and sank into the thirsty soil. The bottle when he recovered it was all but empty, and he propped it back where he'd found it. Then, as he hadn't yet seen the river, obscured from view here by meadow-sweet and willow-herb and clumps of tall yellow irises, he walked along it, looking for a gap; and when he found one he sat down in the rough grass at the water's edge, and took off his shoes and socks, and dabbled his feet. The green water was shockingly cold, and he withdrew his feet quickly and lay back on his elbows, wiggling his toes to dry them. He lay still, with the sun on his face and his eyes shut, and listened contentedly to the watery noises, to a moorhen running along in the reeds, and to a blackbird singing in an alder.

'Better see if they're ready for a cup of tea,' Cecily said to one of her children. And one of her children went ungraciously to do her bidding. Cecily was feeling fraught. She'd spent the afternoon doing the flowers for her dinner party, a task she enjoyed only in theory. Choosing the blooms from the overflow beds in the kitchen garden (the herbaceous border couldn't be raided without upsetting old Goulden, who tended it, and who – because he'd worked there since he was twelve – believed it to be his garden);

185

snipping at *paeonia lactiflora* and geraniums *pratense* and *sanguineum;* filling her trug with – a weed, really, but pretty – the oh so useful *alchemilla mollis,* she'd been distressed by the shrieks and yells and splashes that came to her from over the high brick wall. They were not her children in the pool (its novelty, only two years after installation, had worn off, so that even on the hottest days none of hers entered it now, unless at midnight, fully clothed or naked), but the vicar's unprepossesing brood. Her invitation – 'Do come and swim whenever you like, *please*' – had been accepted verbatim, whenever they liked turning out to be weekday evenings and Saturday and Sunday afternoons.

If Willie'd been there, he'd have got rid of the little buggers, she was thinking crossly as, muzzy with sleep and hung about with picnic things, Gladys and Arnold came into view behind Sophie on the path.

'Ah, there you are!' she said brightly, and then, having enquired about their afternoon, she led them away to the downstairs cloaks.

At tea, laid out under a cedar on the lawn, the Carters were royally attended. 'Another sandwich for Gladys?' and the plate was proffered. 'Arnold – a drop more tea?' and his cup was filled. King Arnold and Queen Gladys sat on cushionless teak thrones, while their subjects sprawled on the grass at their feet.

They were confused at the number of children, but – as Cecily explained with a laugh as she introduced them – they were not all hers and William's. Jamie and Ned for instance, were her nephews (Jamie and Ned raised their hands in a vague salute, and resumed their conversation); Arabella a friend of Sophie's, and staying the weekend ('Hi there,' Arabella said); Jean-Marie was French, and over from Beynac on a month's exchange visit (Jean-Marie followed his 'allo' with a scowl and a shrug). The conversation was confusing too, most of it seeming to do with the video nasty everyone, with the exception of George ('That's George – the little one with red hair,' Cecily said, pointing) and Olivia, had been watching all afternoon. Mungo, whom Arnold and Gladys consciously missed, and who might not have made things easier for them, was still playing cricket – run out second ball, according to George who'd been watching, 'and now, I presume, dropping catches in the outfield.' William was absent also, having been called away ('On a Saturday! It really is uncivilized!' Cecily had exploded) to an unexpected, and urgent, CLA meeting.

'No, really, thank you. That was very nice,' Gladys said, relieved to be rid of her cup. The milk hadn't been fresh, she decided, or else some fish in the fridge had tainted it – her tea had tasted of kippers.

Olivia, who since lunch had been drawing a view of the stables and the downs behind them, now ambled towards them over the lawn.

'How did it go, darling? Let's have a look,' Cecily called. 'Olivia's at art college,' she explained to the Carters. But Olivia's drawing had not gone well, and she frowned and kept her sketch book under her arm.

'Our grandson's an artist,' Arnold said, 'a student, you might say.'

'Oh right. Where?' Olivia asked, not really interested, only half listening.

'Clerkenwell,' Gladys said.

'Camberwell,' Arnold corrected her. 'Or rather (as Olivia and Cecily opened their mouth to reveal their astonishment) he's just left. He got the top award, degree, I think they call it. They's very pleased with him at the college, his Dad says.'

Cecily was dumbfounded. Her daughter Olivia, nearly at the end of her Foundation Course at Trowbridge, had applied to Camberwell and to Chelsea, had gone for interview at St Martin's and the R.A. Schools, and had been turned down by them all.

'We've never had an artist in the family before,' Arnold went on tactlessly, 'we never had nothing like it. But good luck to the lad, I said to his father, good luck to him. More power to his elbow, is what I say.'

'Quite so,' Cecily said faintly. 'How exciting.'

'He goes to the Royal College next,' Arnold seemed bent on

adding insult to terrible injury, 'on some sort of scholarship.'

Tea was over, but the Carters were still sitting there. They were more than ready to leave – the teak chairs were killers, Gladys's bladder was beginning to fill again, and she was worried about the cats who weren't used to being left – but how did you just get up and go? Wouldn't it look rude? She drummed her fingers lightly on the handbag in her lap and gave Arnold a look. At this moment Cecily got up from the grass. It had been a great success, she thought. But enough was enough. She didn't want to chivvy them, but the trouble was those sort of people – and it was *not* their fault – never knew when to leave, never quite knew when to take a hint.

'Do come and see us again,' she said in the drive, bending her head to Arnold's window, 'anytime you're passing. And bring your artist grandson with you – Olivia would be fascinated to meet him, I know!'

Taking a final look at the house, Arnold suddenly got it, the thing that had been bothering him, on and off, all afternoon. Corsham Court! That's what it reminded him of, Corsham Court! Smaller, mind you, and without the entablatures, but similar, definitely similar.

Goodbyes and thankyous over, the Carters did up their seatbelts, a procedure which took a little time because Gladys could never remember how to work hers. Arnold switched on the engine. Nothing happened.

'. . . and it was two hours before their banger would start!' Cecily told the Waddesdons and the Hascombes and the Muckrosses over the quails' eggs. It had been a nightmare, as they could imagine: she couldn't have a bath or change. She couldn't fetch Mrs Gannett (William interrupted at this point, to explain to the Muckrosses, who weren't in the know, that Mrs Gannett was the wonder who 'did' at dinner parties); William was at some dreary meeting ('Not my fault,' William protested, peeling a fourth egg); Mungo, the only one who knew anything at all about motor cars, was busy hitting sixes; the garage, it being a Saturday, was of course shut ('Typical,' Eddie Muckross groaned, 'of this Godforsaken country'); needless to say, they weren't members of the AA or anything like *that* – 'but to give them their due,' she added, because she didn't want to be unfair – she'd liked the Carters, she really had – 'they were hideously embarrased. They didn't know where to put themselves. I suspect they were longing to get back to Swindon – ' Loud laughter greeted this notion.

'Well I feel real sorry for those poor Carters,' the Hascombes' American said. 'Forgive me for asking – but doesn't it seem a little odd of you, to any of you, even a little patronising, maybe, for a baronet and his lady to spend a whole afternoon entertaining – waiting on – the kind of people you would normally employ to wait on you? Don't you have more relevant ways of relating to people from a different socio-economic background? Of breaking down the barriers? Barriers which surely must – if Great Britain is to survive into the twenty-first century – be broken down?'

A silence followed this extraordinary speech. During it, Cecily felt upset. She hadn't thought of her rescue of the Carters in that light, and she knew, she was certain, they hadn't either.

'What's she on about?' Eddie Muckross eventually hissed in Sally Hascombe's ear. 'What does socio-whatsit mean?'

'Class,' Sally Hascombe hissed back. 'Class to you, dearie, class.'

'Love your flowers, Thistle,' said Boo Waddesdon, who'd only that moment noticed them. 'Very, very pritts.' And she leant forward, and stuck her nose in the arrangement.

William, on the American's left, explained to her that she hadn't got it quite right; that the upper classes and the working classes in England really had a lot going for each other; that it had always been so: that there were good historical reasons for this (he did not elucidate) and that it was the people in-between that one simply couldn't get along with, and had nothing to say to; but that was a fact of life; unfortunately.

'Thank you so much, Mrs Gannett, that was delicious,' Cecily

189

said. Mrs Gannett, coming in to clear, had created a timely diversion.

The Carters were forgotten while the salmon was brought in and borne by Mrs Gannett from left elbow to left elbow.

'Everything's cold, I'm afraid,' Cecily apologized.

'Yum yum yum yum,' Archie Hascombe said.

'Does anyone, offhand, know of anyone who's wanting an adorable – slightly runtish, pr'aps – hunt terrier puppy?' Julia Muckross enquired. But offhand, no one did.

During the eating of the salmon, the Waddesdons and the Muckrosses discovered they had sons at the same school, though not in the same house; and the Muckrosses and the Hascombes discovered they had daughters at the same school, though not in the same year – extremely useful to know, they were all agreed, when it came to exeats and doing the run. Later on, it emerged that Archie Hascombe's nephew worked – on the international investment side – in Eddie Muckross's merchant bank; and then Tiny Waddesdon remembered that as a schoolboy he'd had half a rod on old Lord Muckross's water.

'It all sounds like some kind of exclusive club,' the American complained, and they all agreed that yes, in a way, you could say it was.

The American was non-plussed. She'd envisaged at least some cultural debate – a dialogue on the new play at the Theatre Upstairs, maybe, or on the new movie at the Screen on the Hill. Were the British never serious? Were their concerns only schoolchildren and dogs?

Eddie Muckross, sitting opposite, and suddenly noticing her distress, came gallantly to her aid. 'Tell us about life in Noo Jersey, Ma'am,' he encouraged in an over-the-top southern accent, moving a lifesize silver grouse so that he could see her better. 'Dish us the dirt. Give us the low down.'

The pudding arrived, purple, splendidly conical, bleeding blackly into its dish.

'Summer pud – what spoiling, Mrs Gannett!' Tiny Waddesdon

said, beaming up at her as he helped himself. 'Blackcurrants, redcurrants, raspberries, cherries, mulberries – all *sorts* of goodies in there,' he reassured his American neighbour, whose lot it had been to broach the pudding, and who now prodded the sodden bread on her plate uncertainly with a spoon. 'Rather more palatable than pumpkin pie, I think you'll find,' he added.

The arrival of the pudding, and William's getting up to fetch a bottle of what he always referred to as 'noble rot' ('the fungus they apply to the root of the Sauternes vine' Tiny Waddesdon informed his neighbour) reminded Cecily that the best bit of the Carter saga remained untold.

'Hope you appreciate your pudding wine,' she said, as William ('No, no, no, Willie, I've done frightfully well, I can't possibly drink any more,' Boo Waddesdon said, clamping a hand over her glass) walked round the table with the bottle. Her beloved son Mungo–Cecily told them, waving a hand for quiet – who'd been asked to take some beer and plonk to the river to cheer up the Carters' picnic, had by mistake ('On purpose,' William interrupted her) taken a bottle of Willie's best noble rot, and then when Sophie – who'd been sent to fetch them up for tea – got there, she'd found Mrs C. snoring drunkenly on her chair, Albert comatose on the river bank, and the bottle and beer cans empty under the tree. 'The old biddies had drunk the lot!'

Everyone – except the American, and anyway Americans had no sense of humour – laughed, and even William managed a smile. They were still snorting when Mrs Gannett arrived with the coffee tray, and placed it in front of Cecily on the table. Bathed in candlelight and laughter, Cecily considered her day. Not *quite* a fairy-tale ending for the Carters, perhaps (she'd made them promise to ring and let her know they'd got home safely, she remembered – and they hadn't, of course) but she knew they'd really enjoyed their outing.

I'll be able to dine out on it for years, she realized as she passed the cups down the table, and asked Eddie Muckross to give the sugar a shove.